Project Arachne Novellas:
Tsuchigumo

Jeremy Walker Thrillers:
Blue Moon

Blue Moon side-stories:
Kaiju Epoch

Coming Soon:
The Kaiju Titanomanchy

Kaiju Epoch

A Kaiju Thriller

Zach Cole

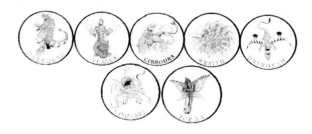

For Justin Snyder, who has been with me on this story through its many iterations, and has been my best friend since 5th grade. Thanks for being there for me man!

WARNING!

THE FOLLOWING STORY CONTAINS SPOILERS OF THE AUTHOR'S PREVIOUS BOOK *BLUE MOON*. IT IS RECOMMENDED THAT YOU READ *BLUE MOON* BEFORE THIS STORY. IF YOU HAVE READ *BLUE MOON* OR JUST DON'T CARE, PLEASE CONTINUE AND ENJOY...

Prologue I:

Ancient Greece

Typhon watched as the green liquid surged through the tube hanging from the ceiling of the facility they set up, into the injector gun where it was squeezed into its host, a prisoner of war, sitting a few feet from the station. Even as the liquid finished being injected into the prisoner's arm, the mutation had already started. Jagged spikes emerged from the creature's back and armor began to form all over its body. In a matter of minutes, the creature was totally transformed into a hideous beast and was growing. Though, it wasn't growing as rapidly as he had hoped it would.

"Looks like we may have to adjust it some more," he said.

"Yes, just a tiny bit," the creature standing beside him, Echidna, said. She was a visitor from the stars that helped make the experiment they were conducting possible with her advanced technology.

The being before him squealed in pain as its body continued to change and grow. Soon, it would be gigantic. He didn't know exactly when it would stop growing, but it would be at a great height, casting a shadow on his enemy.

Humanity.

Ever since their creation, they have been a pain in Typhon's side. His lips formed into a sneer as he thought of the rebellious creatures. He hated them with a passion.

They are a mistake that I plan on correcting very soon, he thought. *These…monsters…will be the tools of their eradication.*

The prisoner before him wasn't the first to have the liquid injected into them. There were others, including himself and Echidna. The Hydra was one such creation. The result of injecting the liquid into a common lizard. The Cyclops was the result of using the liquid on a human subject. Orthrus and Cerberus were the result of using the liquid on canines. They were effective killing machines but they weren't big enough for their purposes. They only ranged around the forty-foot area in height.

The monster growing before them should be big enough, however. Once outfitted with Echidna's advanced weapons, the monster would be an unstoppable weapon. It was now forty-feet tall and growing. The only thing keeping the creature from going on a pain filled rampage were the energy cuffs tethering its wrists to the ground.

Though, he'd be glad to unleash it upon the nearest human city, Athens.

But it was not ready for that yet.

Hyperion, he thought, deciding on a name for the monster. He found it easier to keep track of them if he assigned them names.

Soon Hyperion would be ready, though. Along with the rest of the creatures that would soon follow him. Echidna called them Vexnoxtuque. She said it meant 'monster' in her language. It was an adequate name for the creatures. They were monsters, after all. Mindless killing machines.

"We just need to adjust the serum's growth rate and it should finally be perfected," Echidna said with a clap of her giant hands.

She instructed one of her fellow *starcomers* to adjust the serum. Once they did, they grabbed another prisoner and continued the experiment anew. The prisoner was shackled and injected with the green liquid. Its whole body changed into a completely different being. The serum caused different mutations in each individual, but this was the first time he saw it completely transform a creature into something completely new.

He smiled as the Vexnoxtuque grew rapidly, quickly surpassing Hyperion's height who was now sixty feet tall. The new creature's growth topped out at exactly four-hundred feet, towering high above them.

"Excellent! We have done it! Now, we can continue," Echidna exclaimed with glee, rubbing her clawed hands together.

"Yes, let us bring about humanity's downfall," Typhon said with a wide sharp toothed grin.

Oceanus, Typhon thought, deciding on a name for the new green skinned Vexnoxtuque, its flesh coming alive with hues of reds, yellow, and blues as the sun struck it.

They continued the experiment many more times, creating twelve of the monsters in all: Hyperion, Oceanus, Theia, Mnemosyne, Tethys, Phoebe, Rhea, Themis, Coeus, Crius, Iapetus, and Kronos.

The Titans and Titanesses.

THE HARBINGER

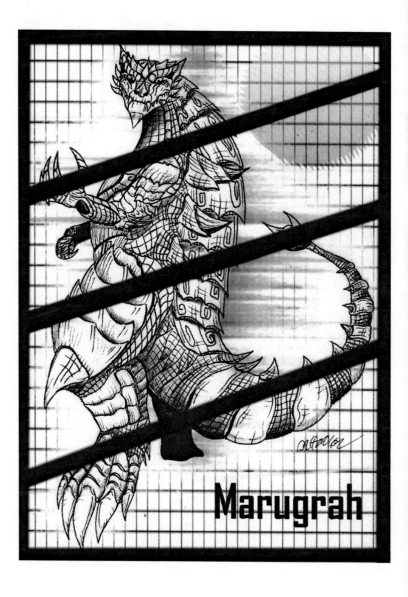

Marugrah

Maruia, Andromeda Galaxy
2017

Marugrah pumped his stubby reptilian legs, running along the path leading to the gleaming ruby red castle. He was dressed scaly head to clawed toe in Maruian Honor Guard armor. It was the armor of the Queen's personal guard. Only the best of the best were picked for the role.

And he was one of the best.

Despite being a three-foot-tall dinosaur-like being, he was a great warrior. He had fought in many battles that would have seemed impossible to leave alive. Yet, he did leave, surviving the impossible. It was what got him to where he was now, by the Queen's side.

His claws squealed across the metal floor as he skidded to a stop in front of the queen's throne.

Marugrah? What is the matter? Marudon, the Queen, asked telepathically, dressed in her royal cloak, ancient Maruian symbols covering it.

Telepathy was the way Maruians communicated to one another and other beings as they lacked any ability to speak with their mouths. They were far from unintelligent, however. Some Maruians would argue that they are one of the smartest species in the galaxy.

That won't last long, however.

I bring terrible news, my Queen, Marugrah said. *Our fear has come true. The monsters ravaging the galaxy are now approaching our home world. They will break our atmosphere momentarily. We must get you to safety.*

The rest of the queen's personal guard piled in behind Marugrah, all reporting the same thing.

The Plagueonians have arrived.

They were a warmonging race of creatures who wanted no more than to conquer other races. They had been making their way from planet to planet. Destroying and enslaving. Marugrah had fought against them on many occasions, trying to help allies from falling to them...to no avail. Everything they did was hopeless against them.

Now they had arrived on Maruia.

The Queen hopped down from her golden throne decorated with various colored jewels, her claws creating an echoing clack as they hit the red floor.

We will escort you to the escape shuttle, Maruchar, the third in command, said. Marugrah is the second in command. Ultimately, the queen usually was head of operations but in a situation like they were being faced with, Marugrah had the say-so.

As they stepped outside, energy lances at the ready, smoke and the sounds of battle overwhelmed them. Their beloved city was being rippled with laser fire from a giant overhead ship.

They have entered the atmosphere already, Marugrah snarled.

Maruian military troops dressed in various armors showing their ranks surge forward, armed with laser rifles and energy swords. A laser blast struck close to the group as they crossed the plaza to the waiting ship but they never flinched. The golden city around them was crumbling and being destroyed. It was a day Marugrah hoped to never see.

Yet, there they were.

The pain filled squeal of a fellow Maruian pulled Marugrah's eyes. A crushed body of twisted scaly flesh and metal laid under a massive armored boot. He looked up the decoratively carved silver armor to the helmeted visored head. A sick smile spread across the creature's exposed face as it brought up a laser rifle in its massive four digit hands, aimed at the eight creature group of Honor Guards surrounding the queen.

Another of the Honor Guards near the back of the circle saw the creature and brought up a laser rifle of his own. He pulled the trigger at the same time the Plagueonian did. The Honor guard's hit the Plagueonian in its armored chest, pushing the creature back. The Plagueonian's shot hit the Guard behind Marugrah who was in front of the Queen, burning a hole in his skull, killing him. The circle around the Queen grew tighter to fill the spot of the fallen Guard.

They knew they could die on this run. It was the price they had to pay for the protection of the Queen. Marugrah said a silent prayer for his fallen brother.

They were almost to the ship when a giant chrysalis shot out of the bottom of the overhead ship. It landed in the city, shaking the ground like an earthquake. It landed behind some of the city's towers, obscuring Marugrah's vision of the pod. Then, the towers ceased to exist as a massive creature swiped its three tails through them, obliterating them.

They reached the ship as the Vexnoxtuque that destroyed the towers let out an angry wail. The Guards helped the Queen into the open side hatch.

Marugrah, you go with her, Maruchar said, pushing Marugrah toward the hatch they helped the Queen in.

This wasn't part of the plan, Marugrah countered, struggling from being put in the ship.

I'm sorry old friend.

Maruchar kicked Marugrah in the ship, sending him tumbling into the cargo bay as Maruchar quickly shut the hatch. Another angry wail from the Vexnoxtuque sprung Marugrah into action, forgetting about his friend going off plan. He had to get the Queen off the planet and out of the Plagueonian's hands. He rushed into the small ship's cockpit and seated himself behind the controls. He worked his clawed fingers across the control board, starting the ship and prepping it for takeoff. With the ship finally ready and the Vexnoxtuque taking up most of the windshield, Marugrah pulled up on the joystick and guided the oval shaped ship up and away from the ground.

Two more chrysalis ejected from the massive ship sitting in Maruia's atmosphere, hitting the ground and releasing two more Vexnoxtuque upon the city. Tanks fired plasma balls at the creatures as they tore apart the city and spread out in different directions where they would make their way across the planet. It was a battle already lost. Marugrah should be taking part in that battle. Maruchar should be where he now sat. The job he now had was more important than the battle below, he knew.

But I have the most experience fighting this enemy, Marugrah's mind told him. He pushed the thought aside, focusing on the task at hand.

Marugrah dodged laser blasts emitted from the big

ship and the smaller ships aiding in the siege. The fire from the ground masked Marugrah and the Queen's escape. Once in orbit, he hesitated a moment, watching the three Vexnoxtuque fight with the failing Maruian army. In a matter of minutes, his home-world had turned into a war zone. If Marugrah was capable of crying, he would at the sight of his dying planet.

He had seen this happen so many times before. It was horrible. But not as horrible as seeing his own home planet turned to ash and his fellow brothers and sisters slaughtered.

We must go this instant, the Queen said, shaking him out of his mourning. He typed in some coordinates, setting course for the nearest habitable planet. A planet called Earth. It had the same atmosphere as Maruia and contained a smart race of creatures called Humanity.

On the short six month ride to Earth, Marugrah and Marudon studied everything they could on the planet's inhabitants. Their history. Their habits. How they treated extraterrestrial life. None of it sounded promising. Humanity was a violent and hardly welcoming race. Every alien species they had come across was harvested and dissected and covered up from public knowledge. Much of the human race didn't even know aliens exist.

But they would.

And Marugrah would be there to stop them this time.

Their ship touched down in a mountain range the humans called 'The Rocky Mountains'. It was an odd name to call mountains. Of course they were rocky. Mountains are made of rock. Marugrah hoped none of the humans saw the ship touch down. He was hiding from them as much as he was the Plagueonians. After a few hours of climbing, Marudon beside him, a chopping sound filled the air. He looked to the blue sky to see an olive colored human aircraft. It was what the humans called a 'helicopter'. It flew overhead, passing them by. Then another did. And another. All heading toward Marugrah's landed ship.

Damn! The humans saw us land, Marugrah cursed.

Marugrah grabbed his Queen's hand as they descended down the mountains to avoid being cut open like livestock to be examined and studied. As far as he knew, they were the last of their kind. They didn't have long before the Plagueonians arrived on Earth. He knew how they were. They wouldn't allow Marugrah and Marudon to escape that easily. The human military wouldn't stand a chance against the giant monsters they use as weapons.

Their technology was very low grade. They used explosive weapons. And something called...nuclear bombs. Those kind of weapons would not be of use against the Vexnoxtuque. Nothing he knew of could hurt one, actually. Well, besides one.

They ran for weeks, ending up on the outskirts of a place called Wooster. They hid in a grove of tall yellow grass just outside a farm. It was night. He stepped out onto the black asphalt road, his head being met with the bumper of a car, knocking his helmet off. His armor scraped against the bottom of the vehicle as it drove over him, skidding to a stop.

Marugrah was barely conscious when two figures stood over him, talking. He felt himself being picked up from the ground as his vision turned to black and his mind faded into unconsciousness.

2

Outskirts of Wooster, Ohio

William Carver sat in the passenger seat of his best
friend Aaron Smith's old Jeep as they drove down the
road on their way home from the Cleveland Comic Con,
Disturbed's *Inside the Fire* blaring from the speakers.
Will watched with amusement as his friend 'rocked out'
to the music, using the steering wheel as a drum and
head banging. It was a somber song, speaking about the
death of one of the singer's girlfriend whom he walked
in to find hung but somehow Aaron found amusement
from it. He sometimes worried that Aaron would get
them into wreck doing this but no one was on the road
they were driving down.

A thud from the front of the car startled them, a
scraping starting from the front of the vehicle and
continuing under the car. Aaron stopped the car, giving
Will a worried look.

"Did we hit something?" Will asked, panicking that
maybe they hit a dog or some poor animal.

"Sounded like it. Whatever it was, it sounded metallic.
I hope it didn't mess up my car," Aaron said, opening
his door.

"That's what you're worried about? Your car? What if
we hit some animal or an actual person?" Will said,
opening his door and stepping out into the cool July
night air.

With no answer from Aaron, he headed toward the
back of the car where a small figure laid. He walked up

to it, producing a small flashlight he randomly picked up at the Con. He shined it on the figure, seeing a small reptile wearing some kind of shiny silver metal armor.

"What the hell?" Aaron asked. "Someone dress up their pet lizard up in a knights' armor?"

"I don't know," Will said, lifting the helmet off the creature and inspecting its red reptilian face. "It doesn't look like any lizard I've ever seen before."

"Maybe it's some kind of new breed or something. People are always inter-breeding species together to try and make new ones."

"A new breed that wears armor? That's so totally plausible."

"It's not like you have any ideas, asshole."

Will chuckled. "Anyways, it could be hurt. We need to get it some help."

He picked the surprisingly heavy creature off the ground with a grunt, carrying it back to the Jeep. He opened the back door, setting the lizard on the back seat. He shut the door and got in the passenger side door he was sitting in before.

Aaron put the car in drive and drove to Will's house. They weren't that far away from it when they hit the lizard. Will carried the creature in his house, setting it on his bed in his bedroom upstairs. His house had three bedrooms but he only used that one, the rest being either empty or used for storage. He didn't even have that much stuff to store, anyways.

"Is it dead?" Aaron asked.

"I don't think so. It's breathing," Will said, pointing at the lizards's scaly sides rising and falling.

Will reached down, unbuckling the straps that held the

armor in place, removing the armor from the creature's body. He piled it on the bed next to the lizard. Free of the armor, the lizard looked more like a small red dragon minus the horns, spikes, and wings.

"Looks like a dragon," Aaron said, mirroring Will's thoughts, excitement filling his eyes. "Dude! Did we just find a frickin' dragon?"

"I think it's a bit small to be a dragon," Will said.

"It could be a baby dragon."

"True. It could be…"

Will was cut off as the creature lying on its side began to stir. It curled into a ball, shivering before uncurling and getting to its three toe, black clawed feet. It looked at Will with its green, diamond shaped pupils then at Aaron, its eyes going wide. It scrambled back against the wall the bed sat against on the far side of the fairly big room.

"Don't hurt me," a voice squealed, making Will and Aaron look around for the source.

"Who said that?" Aaron asked.

They looked back to the only living creature in the room with astonishment, realizing who spoke.

"Did you say that?" Will asked.

"Of course I did," the voice came again but the lizard's mouth didn't move.

"How…? You're not moving your mouth," Aaron said, confused.

My voice is being telepathically projected into your brains, allowing me to communicate with you.

"Incredible," Will muttered.

Y-you're not going to dissect me to figure out how my brain is able to do that, are you?

"What? God, no. That would be horrible. We brought you here because we thought you might be hurt."

No. I am fine. Just a little sore from being hit by your mechanical transportation.

"Sorry about that. Didn't see you on the road," Aaron said, rubbing the back of his neck in embarrassment. "If you're alright, I'm going to get going. It's late and I need sleep."

"Alright, see you dude," Will said, escorting the man out. He then went back to his room, seeing the lizard-dragon-creature inspecting its armor.

You took my armor off? it asked.

"Yeah, I did. I thought maybe it would maybe make you more comfortable," Will replied.

Personally, I am more comfortable in the armor. I've worn it for millennia.

"Millennia? Without taking it off? That sounds kinda gross. Do you guys even bathe...Wait. Just how old are you? What are you?"

I am a Maruian. What humans would call an alien. I am from the planet Maruia. And I am 50,000 years old. No, we do not bathe. Our bodies are the cleanest in the galaxy. Liquids seep from underneath our scales, washing away any dirt or other contaminants from our bodies. As for my name, it is Marugrah, Guard of...Queen...Marudon...

The lizard, Marugrah, stopped as if realizing something. He let out grunts and growls, looking as if he was scalding himself. He frantically searched the room, looking for something.

"What is it?" Will asked.

My Queen. I was with her when your friend's

motorized vehicle hit me. Did you recover her as well? he asked.

"Uh, no. Just you."

Marugrah let out an angry growl, baring his teeth and making Will reach for his baseball bat located behind his book case. He didn't need to draw it, though, as Maru help up his tiny clawed hands, looking as if he was calming himself.

We need to find her immediately. We must return to the place I was hit. She may be waiting there for me, he said.

"Are you serious. That was a mile away. I'm not walking there at night. I'm exhausted as it is," Will countered.

If we do not go now, she will be gone.

"Sorry, man. I need sleep. I have work in the morning."

Marugrah hissed angrily.

"You know, for an alien, you're kind of a dick," Will said.

You do not understand the importance she is to me, Maru growled.

"Fine, we'll go find your girlfriend. Come on," Will growled back, rolling his eyes.

She is not...my mate, he said as they made their way downstairs to the living room where Will picked up a giant backpack. Maru looked at it with disgust.

"Get in," Will said.

What? No way, Maru snapped.

"Dude, we're taking my bike. I can't hold you and operate it at the same time."

Ugh, fine.

Maru slipped into the bag and Will hefted it up, sliding the straps over his shoulders.

For the record, you need to clean this thing out. It's quite dirty, Maru said, his head peeking out of the bag as Will walked outside toward his bike that was leaning against the side of the house.

"I'll keep that in mind," he replied, readying the bike and hopping on it.

It took them an hour to reach the spot where Aaron and Will hit Maru. By the time they reached their destination, Will was exhausted, but forced himself to stay awake.

Maru jumped from the bag, diving into the bushes on the side of the road. Will watched the bushes shift as Maru rooted through them, letting out guttural barks. He searched for ten minutes before emerging, looking defeated.

She's not here, he said somberly.

"Well that's just great. We came up here for no reason," Will muttered.

She probably thinks I'm dead. We need to find her.

"Yeah, well not tonight, dude. We're going home and I'm going to sleep for as long as I can. I have work tomorrow."

I need to find her.

"Then stay out here and look for her by yourself. I am going home with or without you."

Will started to push away on his bike but was stopped by Maru's voice.

Wait, wait. I'll come with you. But...only if you help me find my Queen. I mean...I need a place to stay for now. And you're the only human I think I can trust.

"Smart man...er...lizard," Will said with a smile as Maru climbed back into the backpack.

3

Four Months later...
Wooster, Ohio

Will walked out of the cold November air and into the warmth of the coffee shop, the bell above the door letting out a ding, announcing his arrival to the cashier, a girl with golden brown hair in a loose ponytail, beautiful blue eyes, and a heartwarming smile. She was the reason he always chose to come to this small coffee shop instead of the Starbucks uptown. That and the ridiculous prices Starbucks had on coffee. He couldn't afford spending the money on coffee they charged. As for the girl, he could never work up the courage to ask her out. Ashley Singer was her name, he believed.

"Um, just a black coffee, thanks," Will said, digging into his pocket for the money to pay for his order.

"Just black? Well, aren't we a tough guy," Ashley said, her face in an expression he wasn't accustomed to Flirtation maybe? Her voice, however, was full of sarcasm. Was she mocking him?

His only response was an awkward laugh, not knowing what else to respond with. He set the money on the counter and slid it to her.

"So tell me something," she said, putting the money in the register and then looking up, making eye contact with him. "Are you actually going to drink it today?"

"H-huh?"

"Come on dude. You come in here and order a coffee every day, then you go sit down at that table over there and stare at the wall. You're cute and all, but a guy can only do that for so long before it starts to look weird."

"I didn't think you noticed."

"It would be hard not to."

"I guess I look like a total creeper now and have ruined any chance I might have had of you liking me then, huh?"

"Nah. I've seen you come in here with your friends. I don't actually think you're a weirdo but I could be wrong. You should probably ask me out before I change my mind about you."

She gave Will a wink, getting a less awkward and more honest laugh out of him this time.

"I can assure you, I am no weirdo creeper. I promise. You...you wanna go see a movie?" he said with a smile.

"Sure. I get off in ten," she replied with a smile of her own, sending butterflies fluttering madly around his stomach.

Ten minutes later, they walked across town, hand-in-hand to Will's house on their way to the downtown movie theater. They walked down the slanted asphalt road, around a corner, past the green neighboring house and into the concrete driveway that also led to an abandoned trailer behind the wooden fenced, overgrown backyard. They walked up the wooden stairs leading to the wooden porch that was built over the concrete slab that used to serve as the porch before. His house wasn't much. Just a regular two story, light blue house. It was too big for him really, being a three-bedroom house, but it was cheap and he needed a house at the time so he got it. It was a fixer upper and he did his best to fix it up. It still wasn't the best, though.

He opened the white front door to his house and turned to Ashley.

"I've just got to run in and take care of something before we go," he told her.

"So you're *not* going to invite me in?" she asked him, a solitary eyebrow raised.

"Well, I didn't wanna be too forward."

"It's cold out here, dude."

"Right. Yeah. You can come in if you'd like."

Will walked into the house, a living room beyond the door where a television and recliner chair resided, a kitchen beyond the living room. Will headed toward the kitchen.

"Awesome," Ashley muttered, her face deadpan as she stepped inside the house.

Will walked into the kitchen, obscuring his vision of the beautiful young woman. Although being twenty years old, he was never...'good with the ladies' as they say these days. He had maybe two girlfriends in his life and that was maybe five years ago. Being on a date now felt surreal to him.

He opened the refrigerator door, finding the left over burger from the night before and grabbed it.

"Well, so far, we have walked halfway across town and you have made me stand in the cold. Way to kick off a first date," Ashley said from the living room.

"Yet, you're still here. I must be really cute, then," Will said, throwing the burger in the microwave with a chuckle. He turned to see a blur speed from the stairs leading to the upstairs that is connected to the kitchen. The blur jumped up on the table, rubbing his scaly clawed hands together.

You're home early, Marugrah observed, speaking to Will inside his head.

"So, what was so important that we had to stop here before going to the movies?" Ashley asked, still out of his sight.

You brought a girl here? Marugrah asked, his voice in his head sounding a little disappointed.

"Just so I could feed you," he told him.

"I had to feed Maru," he said to Ashley.

"What the hell is a Maru?"

"He's my pet."

Whatever she said next was blocked out by Maru's next words to him.

I am not your pet, Maru said, angry.

"What was I supposed to tell her? You're an alien from another world trying to hide from the U.S. military that seized your ship, while trying to find your Queen that you were separated from when my friend hit you with his car," Will whispered back.

True. But she will be a distraction. We can't afford distractions in the search for my Queen. You should ditch her.

Ashley walked into the kitchen, cutting off their conversation. Her eyes looked from Will to the three-foot-tall red, scaly saurian sitting on the counter. Maru gave her a squinty eyed glare with his green, diamond pupiled eyes.

"So. That's a Maru," she said after a few moments of

staring at Maru.

"Yeah. That's Maru," Will said, walking over to the beeping microwave and removing the burger.

"What is it? Like a komodo dragon or something? Is it even legal to have those as pets?" she asked, still staring at Maru.

"No, no. He's not a komodo dragon. Those are illegal to have, not to mention very venomous. I have no idea what kind of lizard he is. I found him a couple months ago when my friend and I were on our way back from...a thing. We were in his car when we hit the poor little guy in the street. He didn't have an owner so I've been taking care of him ever since," he explained to her. Maru rolled his eyes at the 'poor little guy part'.

"How do you know he doesn't have an owner? Like, do these things wear collars or something?"

"Nope. He doesn't wear a collar."

"Then how…"

I told him, alright. Jeez, Maru barked, annoyed.

"Oh, okay. You can talk..." Ashley said, not moving a muscle.

They stood there in silence for what seemed to Will like hours. This confrontation could scare her away and then no more date. That actually scared Will. He really liked this girl...

"I feel like you could have started off with that," she said, confusing him.

She isn't freaked out by this, Will thought.

You're right. Maybe we got off on the wrong foot, Maru says, extending his clawed hand to her. *Hi, I'm Marugrah. Nice to meet you.* He did his best at a smile, exposing his sharp teeth to her.

"I would but you're sort of scaly and gross. No offense," she said, not moving from her place in the kitchen doorway.

None taken, Maru said, turning to Will.

I don't like her. You should totally ditch her, he said, projecting his voice only into Will's mind.

"I'm not going to ditch her," Will said, offended and looking up at Ashley whose eyebrows were raised. "Besides, I really like her. She'll come around. And so will *you.*"

Maru blows out air from his nostrils at the end of his square snout, making a 'hmph' sound. He snatched the burger from Will's hand and ran up the stairs to Will's room where he spent most of his time.

Will turned to Ashley with a shrug. "Ready to go?"

"It's about time," she said with a smile. "What was that about ditching me?"

"Maru kept trying to get me to ditch you."

"I'm glad you're not." She smiled at him.

He smiled back.

Relieved that the encounter with Marugrah hadn't scared her away, Will walked to the door and opened it for her. She giggled as she walked out the door, Will following her. They made their way to the movie theater downtown, laughing and sharing stories.

"You have a pretty nice house for a cashier," she said, walking up the street to the movie theater, Will's hand in hers. "Not to mention it has two extra bedrooms that I'm sure you don't even use."

"Yeah, well, it is cheap rent-wise, mostly cuz it was a dump when I first got it. It's hard to find a house with the money I make that I can afford and still be able to pay bills and food," he replied.

"Yeah, I get that. I'm sorta in the same boat. It certainly is stressful."

"It very much is. I kinda hate having to have to grow up," Will chuckled.

"Yeah, I agree. So, do you walk everywhere?"

"Pretty much, yeah. When you live in the heart of the city, I find you don't have much need for a car. Not to mention I can't afford one right now."

"That is understandable but what if you want to go up to the north end? I mean, that's where most people hang out, not to mention that's where the *good* movie theater is."

"Usually, one of my friends will give me a ride, then, if not, I ride my bike."

"The same ones I see you with at the coffee house?"

"Yeah, we're all really close. I suppose you could say we're like family, brothers. I'll have to introduce you sometime."

They stopped, arriving at their destination. The sign over the entrance read 'Big Picture Movie Theater'. It was a medium sized brown brick building that held only two screening rooms.

"Enough about me. What about you?" Will asked, looking up at the theater's sign.

"What do you wanna know?" Ashley asked.

"Everything that you'd feel comfortable telling me."

"That might take a while."

"I've got all night."

"Maybe more than one 'all night'."

A smile spread across Will's face as he looked into her eyes. "Are you saying you want a second date?"

24

She gave him a wink. "Depending on how good this movie is."

As they walked through the glass double doors leading inside the theater, a thought occurred to Will. Halfway across the room to the main desk where they would buy their tickets, he turned to Ashley.

"We aren't actually going to watch the movie are we?" he asked.

"You're actually really cute," she said with a squinty eyed smile.

4

Washington D.C.

After being separated from her Guard, Marugrah, Marudon, Queen of Maruia, and possibly the last of her kind, was found herself. She ended up passed out on a woman's doorstep. A woman in the human military of all things. She thought the woman would take her to a place to be dissected but instead she took her to a place consisting of creatures and humans. The creatures weren't aliens but they weren't human either. It was a place that hunted down trouble making monsters. It was the perfect place to help prepare for the coming invasion.

She projected the last moments she saw of her home planet into the woman's head. The Plagueonian's ship raining down lasers. The Vexnoxtuque. The death of hundreds in a matter of minutes. She understood the magnitude of the situation and brought it to the attention of the head of the CCU (Creature Counter Unit). It wasn't much of a widely known government agency, but from what Marudon understood, the organization was created after an incident in Fresno, California. Some creatures were recorded there and after seeing their lethality, and demise, the CCU was created to combat any further threats like that.

And just in time.

The people in charge were skeptical at first, but Marudon projected the images into their heads and they saw it as a real threat to their planet. Now, they prepared for the coming war.

"Ma'am!" a man called out, running into Jessica Evangeline's, the woman who found Marudon, bunk which she resided in when she couldn't make it home. She was a part of Gamma squad, one of the many field teams within the CCU. She was what the humans called a Delta Operator before being recruited into the CCU, which consisted of the best of the best. Most of the soldiers have had encounters with supernatural creatures even before coming to the military. The others saw the monsters from Fresno. The CCU was only a few months old so there were only seven teams so far. Alpha, Beta, Charlie, Delta, Echo, Foxtrot, and Gamma. However, more were being recruited soon.

"What is it?" Jessica asked, standing from the bed she and Marudon sat on.

"Satellite sensors have picked up an object heading for Earth. So far it is only on the fringe of Mars but we are getting an image via a space telescope soon. Also, we have picked up traces of the Maruian you have been looking for in Ohio," the man explained.

Are you sure? Have you located Marugrah? Marudon asked, excited that Marugrah may still be alive. When first arriving at the CCU HQ, she made a device that would allow them to track down Marugrah. They would need him if they were to survive the coming Plagueonian invasion.

"We haven't got an exact location yet. We're working on that," the man said. "Cole wants you two in the control room, ASAP."

Cole. Lance Cole. He was head of the CCU. Marudon had never met the man, but she heard soldiers saying he was a fair and honorable man. A fellow soldier at one point in his life, serving in the army. She also heard them say he used to be the Director of the CIA as well.

Marudon hopped down from the bed onto the metal floor with a clunk as her claws struck it. Jessica's room didn't have carpeting just yet. She followed Jessica out of the bunk room and down a long corridor lined with doors. They entered a room at the end of the hall on the right hand side. The room is dark and full of screens with a giant screen near the front. The control room was what they called "that" room.

"Image is ready, ma'am," a woman in front of one of the smaller screens said.

"Pull it up," Christina Angel, leader of fire-team Gamma, said. She was a stern woman, with close cut blonde hair, a tomboy physique, and big arm muscles. Currently, those muscled arms were folded behind her back. An expression that Marudon had seen many military humans make.

Being such a small creature, Marudon had to weave

her way around the work stations to get a good view of the giant screen and the images of the approaching object. The screen showed the real time image of the planet Mars, a red ball of rock in the Milky Way galaxy. It took her a moment to find the aberration moving through the blackness of space. It blended in well as it was grey in color.

"Zoom in on it," Christina said before Marudon could.

The image shifted, zooming in on the object and bringing it into focus. Marudon immediately recognized it. And panicked.

Vexnoxtuque, Marudon muttered, scrabbling backwards and bumping into Christina's legs.

"Vex...nox...tuke?" she asked, sounding out the word. "What is a Vexnoxtuque?"

A Plagueonian weapon. They were originally habitants of other planets that were experimented on and turned into monsters of mass destruction, Marudon explained, composing herself and smoothing out the wrinkles in her royal cloak.

"The image doesn't look like a monster," Jessica said, looking at the image of the silver cylindrical object.

That is just the pod that transports the creature within. The Plagueonians won't be too far behind the Vexnoxtuque.

"A harbinger," Christina muttered.

Exactly.

"Great. How do we stop a Vexnoxtuque?"

You can't. Nothing we know can pierce a Vexnoxtuque's thick hide. My military, the most advanced in the galaxy, has even failed against them. I doubt anything your primitive army has will have any more effect against them. No offense.

"None taken. So, what? We're hopeless against this thing?"

That is what I am saying, yes. But if we can find my guard, Marugrah, he may know what to do. He has faced one of these creatures before. He may know how to kill it. I have heard stories that he managed to kill one.

"We're on it. We have a team tracking Maruian DNA with those devices you rigged up from your ship as we speak. Miss Boyd, track the Vexnoxtuque pod. I want to know where it will land so we can properly greet it."

"Yes, ma'am," the woman behind the computer, Miss Boyd, said, working her fingers over a keyboard.

"Patch us into the search team as well."

"Roger."

The image on the screen shifted from the zoomed in image of the approaching pod to an image displaying names and pictures of the other three members of fire-team Gamma who were in Ohio, tracking down Marugrah.

"Gamma One, progress report," Christina said into her throat mic.

"We've tracked the Maruian DNA signature to a town called Wooster. We're sweeping the town now," Gamma One's Australian accented voice came through a speaker somewhere in the room.

"Report in when you have found him, but take no action until I give the order. We don't want to freak him out. He already thinks we are creatures who only want to cut him up and steal his tech."

"Roger that. Gamma One out."

5

Wooster

Will walked into his room, seeing Maru on his bed, a half-eaten burger beside him and reading some sort of magazine. He only glanced at the image so he didn't see much as his mind was aflutter with other stuff. Until Marugrah said something.

Naked humans are much uglier than clothed humans, Marugrah says, looking up from the magazine.

Seeing the magazine in Maru's hands for what it was, Will lunged forward, ripping it from Maru's clawed hands.

"Where the hell did you get this?" Will shouted, embarrassed, holding the magazine up by one hand.

Under your bed. Why do you have a magazine of human reproduction under your bed? Maru asked with a snicker.

"That is none of your business!"

You humans are quite weird; you know that?

"Think of us however you want."

Will put the magazine on top of a tall bookcase, where Maru couldn't reach it.

So, how'd it go? Judging by the stupid smile you had when you first walked in, something good happened, Maru's eyes lit up and he jumped to his feet. *Please tell me you ditched her!*

"Oh, shut up," Will said, tossing his red jacket at Maru after he took it off. Nothing, not even Maru's sour personality, could ruin Will's good mood. "There is no way I'd be happy about ditching her. Something good did happen, though."

What? Maru asked, peeking out from under the jacket. *Wait... you two didn't...*

"Procreate? No! Kiss? Maybe a little bit. Or a lot."

Did you two even watch the movie?

Will just smiled as he sat on his bed, next to Maru. Maru jumped to the floor, laying in the bundle of blankets that served as his bed.

You disgusting whore. I don't know how you're going to sleep tonight, Maru said, disgusted. He made a barfing sound as he laid on his back on the blankets, expressing his disgust.

"Like a baby," Will said, drifting off to sleep after collapsing onto his bed.

A golden city of towers hovered over Will. He looked around, seeing small reptilian creatures as they went about their daily business, driving around in what looked like hovering vehicles or walking around, wearing colorful cloaks.

Where am I? Will asked himself.

Suddenly, a giant whale-shaped ship with alien symbols carved into its hull descended from the green sky, immediately raining down laser fire on the city. Some struck the citizens, vaporizing them. Others struck buildings, making them crumble to the ground, debris crushing more of the city's inhabitants. The ones that survived began to panic, running for cover as they let out high pitched squeals. A laser stuck close to Will, making him dive for cover as debris flew into the air. He stumbled to his feet, looking back up to a giant ship hovering above him. A hatch on the ship's bottom opened up and fired off some kind of oval missile into the city.

The missile landed in between some towers, out of Will's view. Plumes of dust erupted from the crash site, rolling through the city and over Will, stinging his eyes. A roar unlike anything he had ever heard filled the air. He could only describe it as the roar of an alien lion with an electronic echo to it. The smoke cleared, revealing the creature that made the sound. A massive head rose over the towers, looking as if it was wearing another creature's skull. A yellow oval was located on the creature's skulled snout, shining brightly. Vertebrae like armor plates ran down the creature's back to its three whip-like tails, each ending in four bony prong-like protrusions with a red circle in the middle of them. It looked to stand on four legs. It spun, whipping its tails around, destroying towers. Then, as if it had gone mad, the monster started swatting and clawing at the city with its massive armor plated arms, a giant spike jutting from the creature's shoulder. It let out another anger filled roar.

What the hell is that? Will wondered, horrified at the beast before him.

A Vexnoxtuque, Maru said, suddenly beside him.

A what now? Will tried to ask but it came out as a thought.

We're in a dream, we can't talk physically, Maru said, addressing Will's concern. *As for the Vexnoxtuque, they are weapons. Beings from other planets conquered by the Plagueonians who were experimented on and turned into monsters. We call them Vexnoxtuque.*

Giant monsters... We call those Kaiju on Earth.

Kaiju...I have heard that word in a few comic books you have. Fantastical creatures of large size. Like Godzilla. And Nemesis.

Two more pods shot out from the bottom of the ship, rocket to the ground, and release two more horrifying creatures. One looked like a giant armored spider creature. Eight eyes sit atop a rounded face, its mouth lined with razor sharp teeth. Mandibles jut out of the sides of the creature's mouth. Curved plates of overlapping armor line the creature's back, three thin spines occupying the edges of each individual plate of armor. A stinger of some sort jutted out of the creature's backside. Its underside was alive with hundreds of long, white tentacles matching the creature's skin. Its eight legs were covered in armor, ending in sharp spikes. Its flesh seemed to give off some sort of ghostly energy. It turned its armored head to the sky, letting out a deep warbling sound that Will figured was its roar.

The second creature looked like a walking rose mixed with a venus fly trap. Pink rose petals surround the creature's oval shaped, thorn covered head. Its mouth was lined with hundreds of thorns that probably acted like teeth for the creature. Two leaf-like structures protruded from the monster's back. Its body looked to be made of bundles of vines. Six tendrils with bubble-like pockets extended from the Vexnoxtuque's upper body. Its four legs were stocky and trunk-like, each ending in toe-like structures.

The two new Kaijus go about helping the first, destroying the city and devouring its inhabitants.

This is absolutely horrible. I can't watch this, Will

said, turning away from the horrifying sight.

This is what will happen to your planet, as it did with mine as you are seeing now, Marugrah said. *The Plagueonians are coming. I can feel them.*

How am I even seeing this? Will asked.

Maruians' telepathy sometimes project memories during sleep to others. Dreams even. It's hard for anyone other than a Maruian to tap into. It seems your disgustingly good mood has somehow let you accidently tap into it.

You've never talked about this.

Well, it's not something I like to talk about, considering it is the last moments I saw of my home world.

Ah... Right...

The beeping of an alarm clock roused Will from his sleep. Will raised his head from his pillow, drool leaking from his mouth. He wiped the sleep out of his grey-blue eyes and ran a hand through his brown hair. He rolled from his stomach onto his back, lashing out his arm at the alarm clock. After a few hits, he managed to shut off the alarm. Images of the dream came back to him. The destruction. The slaughter. The monsters. He glanced over at Maru, still asleep atop the bundle of blankets that served as his bed. It was his idea, not Will's. He said it 'felt more like his bed back home'.

Whatever that meant, Will thought.

Then the memories of his date flooded into his mind next, making him smile. He'd go visit her at the coffee shop today. He just hoped he wouldn't seem too...what was the word...needy? Clingy? He didn't know for sure.

He just knew he didn't want to screw anything up with her.

Will swung his legs over the side of his bed, standing up. He looked down at himself, seeing that he was still wearing the same clothes from the previous day. He quickly changed into some fresh clothes before throwing on his red jacket. He quietly made his way out of the room, deciding not to wake up Maru. He walked down the stairs, through the kitchen and living room, out the door and into the cold, morning air. He walked across town, down streets and alleys, finally coming to the coffee shop. He opened the door and stepped inside the coffee house like it was just any other time that he had done it before.

"Hey, handsome. I got your coffee already made for you," Ashley said, a smile on her face, standing behind the counter and holding up a steaming Styrofoam cup.

"You know me well," Will said with a smile of his own as he walked to the counter, pulling out the money from his pocket and holding it out to her. She grabbed ahold of his hand, looking into his eyes. She pulled him partially over the counter by his hand, grabbing the back of his head as she planted her lips on his. Will wasn't expecting that, and neither were the other girls working in the back.

"Oh my gosh, Ash!" one of the girls yelped, surprised at the sight.

"Uh, wow," Will said, dumbfounded as their faces separated. She gave him a wink and a smile as she took the money. He walked over to his usual spot in the corner of the establishment and sat down. He glanced over to the counter seeing Ashley and a girl talking, the girl glancing over at him.

She must be telling her about our date last night, Will thought. He didn't blame her. It was one of the best nights of his life.

His phone rang. He pulled the device out of his pocket and looked at the screen, looking at the LED lit screen showing the caller's identity. Aaron. He hit the answer button and put it to his ear.

"Hey, man," he said into the phone.

"Yo! What are you doing today?" Aaron asked enthusiastically.

"Nothing really. Just at the coffee shop right now."

"Spying on that chick again?"

"N-no! We actually went on a date last night. We saw a movie."

"What! Why didn't you tell me? You should bring her over later! Walt, Jamie, and Nicole are all coming over later. Was calling to see if you wanted to hang with us. We're going to be playing Mario Cart!"

"Yeah, of course I do, man! I am the Mario Cart champion, after all." Will chuckled in a mock 'muahaha'.

"Yeah, yeah. Don't get too cocky. Don't forget your girlfriend. Maybe she can actually beat you at this game."

"What? I'm undefeatable! And I'll see if she wants to. Later man."

He hung up the phone just as Ashley walked over. She set down a bagel and some packets of butter. Will looked up at her questioningly.

"It's on the house, courtesy of me," she said.

"You didn't have to," he said, flattered.

"Don't worry about it."

"Hey, what are you doing later?"

"You want our second date already?"

Will chuckled. "Would that be so bad? But no. Or kind of. I dunno. I mean, my friends are all getting together later and I was wondering if you'd like to come join us."

"Oh...yeah, sure. That sounds nice."

"Awesome! Umm...I mean, great. Glad to hear."

They smiled at each other a moment before going their separate ways.

6

Jake Walker, callsign Gamma One on this mission, looked at the gold, alien device's screen in his hands built by Marudon from scraps within the ship she arrived in. It showed the massive amounts of Maruian DNA in the town, as if the creature had been all over it.

Was the creature running loose in the town? he wondered. If so, tracking him down would be very difficult. Then he spotted a young man leaving a coffee shop which was giving off readings. As soon as the man stepped out of the shop, the device went crazy. The man was giving off some serious Maruian signatures. Could Marugrah disguise himself as a human being? Probably not. He might somehow be associated with Marugrah, however. Trace amounts on his clothes, maybe. Walker had no idea. But maybe he had just found a way to find Marugrah.

"Gamma One to command," Walker said into his throat mic that was barely visible with his casual clothes that made him look like just another citizen of Wooster. His Aussie accent, however, gave him away.

"This is command, go ahead Gamma One," Christina Angel, leader of fire-team Gamma and head of the mission since Marudon is attached to their team, said through his perfectly disguised ear bud.

"We have spotted a young man, about twenty years old, a shit ton of Maruian DNA signatures radiating from him."

"Roger that. Follow but do not approach until I give the order. He may lead us to Marugrah."

"Copy that, ma'am. Exactly what I was thinking."

Walker looked back to the two other men with him, Alicio Brice and Damen Hlad, who were not too pleased with the orders they were just given. They wanted to end this mission, as did Walker. But orders were orders. And with the information they were given from Marudon, a shit storm of hell was heading toward Earth and Marugrah may be the only hope of surviving it. So they followed the young man across town, following him to a light blue house. Walker and his men watched from the hill overlooking the house as the man walked into the house. He emerged a half hour later, this time carrying a backpack on his back which gave off a lot stronger signal than the man himself did. They followed the man back to the coffee shop. He doesn't leave there for another three hours where he was accompanied by a young woman.

The man and woman walked to another house, well more like a trailer. The man knocked on the door and was greeted by another, more enthusiastic young man. Walker pulled out a listening device, listening to their conversation. However, it was nothing more than antagonistic banter and jokes before he led them into the trailer.

"Gamma One to command," Walker said into his mic.

"Go ahead Gamma One," command said.

"There is a large Maruian signature coming from the back pack the boy is wearing. I think he may have Marugrah in it."

"Roger that. Approach cautiously and non-threateningly. Do not pull your weapons. I repeat, do not use any weapons."

"Copy that, Gamma One out."

This is going to be bloody hard, he thought, formulating a plan.

He turned toward the two men. "Alright, here is the plan. I'll go knock on the door and confirm visual contact. You two stay back and wait for my signal if I can't make a friendly introduction. Despite what command said, we may have to use...extreme measures to get them to come with us."

They nodded, knowing the situation. Walker walked up to the door and knocked, hoping it wouldn't come to the extreme measures. They were just kids, after all...right?

7

Will knocked on the door to Aaron's house, a trailer

home on Old Columbus Road. The door swung open, revealing Aaron wearing a hoodie sweatshirt, a black beanie and blue jeans. A stupid grin spread across his stubble covered face, his eyes lighting up behind his round glasses at the sight of them.

"So you convinced her to come, huh?" Aaron beamed.

"I didn't convince her. I asked her and she said yes. Simple as that," Will retorted.

"Sure, sure. Come on in, love birds."

"Tweet, tweet," Will said sarcastically as Aaron ushered them inside the house. They were greeted by Aaron's half-border collie half-no-one-knows dog, Ozzie. He licked both of their hands, getting excited by the arrival of new people, before Aaron told him to calm down and go lay down. Will surveyed the living room. Walt Rogers and Nicole Rivers were sitting on the floor, playing Mario Cart on the big flat screen TV. Jamie Collins was sitting in a chair, his guitar in his arms. Will ushered Ashley over to the couch, setting the back pack that he had been carrying on the couch and opened it up. Maru jumped out of the bag and onto the grey carpeted floor of Aaron's living room, crouching onto all fours and stretching.

Ugh. I hate being in that thing, Maru groaned.

"Yeah, well it's the only way to safely get you around. You don't want the Men in Black or some government agent looking for you to see you now, do you?" Will asked.

No. I want to live, thank you very much.

Will sat down, patting the empty couch beside him, looking up at Ashley whom looked unsure about everyone around her. She giggled and sat down beside him, scooting closer to him.

You two are disgusting, Maru scoffed and scampered off somewhere.

Probably went to socialize with the dog, Will thought with a mental chuckle.

"Awe, look at the happy couple," Nicole said, pushing her long black hair out of her face. With her green eyes and attractive features, she was a pretty girl but Will didn't think she was ever into him. Like everyone else in the room, she was a long-time friend. He had known her since kindergarten. Same with Aaron and Walt. Jamie was one of Aaron's friends, so he had only known him a few years.

"We've only been together a day now. We're still getting to know each other," Ashley said, grabbing Will's thigh and making him jump. "See. I just learned something new."

"Hey!" Will grumbled, his face turning red.

"You certainly know how to make him jump," Nicole laughed, amused with Will's embarrassment.

At least she is getting comfortable with these guys quickly, he thought, watching as she broke out into laughter herself.

A knock on the door broke off her laughter and turned everyone's attention toward the door.

"You expecting someone else?" Jamie asked, looking at Aaron, scratching his spiked brown hair. He scratched his closely shaved chin next, raising an eyebrow over his brown eye. It was a habit Will noticed when Jamie was nervous about something. Something had him on edge.

"Everyone I invited is here," Aaron said, shrugging.

"Who could it be, then?" Will asked quizzically.

Aaron shrugged again, walking over to the door and opening it to a man in a black sweat shirt and black sweat pants. He looked like any regular person passing by. Maru seemed to know better. Will saw him take one look at the man and jump behind the couch.

A man in black! he squealed.

"Can I help you?" Aaron asked the man, his voice switching from his normal sarcastic tone to his rarely used serious tone.

"Um, yeah. Was that a lizard I just saw run under your couch?" the man asked in an Australian accent.

Aaron gave the man a weird look. "What if it was, weirdo?"

"I need to talk to him?"

"Talk to him? You can't talk to a lizard, man."

"Well, you can. They just won't talk back. To a normal lizard, at least. But you and I both know that that is no ordinary lizard, young man."

Everyone in the room stopped what they were doing, ready for a confrontation. Now that Will got a good look at his face, he could tell the man was no ordinary citizen. The accent kind of gave him away, too. But his face had soldier written all over.

"Just who the hell are you? A Man in Black? Here to take him to be experimented on?" Will growled, standing from the couch.

"Heavens no. I'm with the CCU. We need his help. We have his...Queen, Marudon. She made us these," he held up a gold device with a screen on it, "which helped us track down Marugrah."

Maru peeked out from behind the couch, studying the device.

"How do we know she made it and not you," Will asked.

Because humans aren't capable of making that device in the time they made it. He could have forced my Queen to make it, though, Maru said, skeptical.

"I can have a call made to her if you don't believe me," the man said.

I like that option. Please do that.

"Do it," Will said, enforcing Maru's request more forcefully.

The man pulled a phone from his pocket, ignoring the threat in Will's voice, and dialed a number. He greeted the person on the other line via a video chat and stated the situation he was in before holding the phone out. Aaron grabbed the phone and handed it to Will. The screen was of a woman who had the cold face of a soldier, like the man standing at the door, with brown hair pulled back into a pony tail and a creature like Maru wearing a jeweled helmet that covered the top of its face, a red cloak covered in alien symbols covering its body. He crouched down beside Maru, allowing him to be in the screen, too.

"Hello," the woman said with a warm smile that almost seemed impossible for a soldier. "I am Jessica Evangeline. I found Marudon a few months ago. As you both can see, she is unharmed and free to do as she likes. Instead, she has chosen to stay with us to help us get ready for the coming invasion. The situation is dire, Marugrah." At the last part, the woman's voice changed to a deeper octave. She was not in control of those last words.

"What is the situation, my Queen," the words coming

out of Will's mouth deep as well, indicating they were not his own. He didn't fight it as he knew whose they were.

"A Vexnoxtuque is currently on its way here to Earth. It should touch down within the hour in a major human city," Jessica said in a deep voice.

"That means the Plagueonians aren't far behind," Will said with the same deep voice.

"We need you here as soon as possible. We must get ready for the coming attack. We need to find a way to kill the Vexnoxtuque."

"Killing a Vexnoxtuque is impossible. The only way to kill a Vexnoxtuque is with another Vexnoxtuque. Where are we going to get one of those? Are we going to build a machine to make one?"

"Of course not! That is abhorrent to even think of. Why? Have you done it?"

"No. I just hijacked a control device and was somehow able to fix it to the back of the creature's head. I used it to kill another. That is how I killed one. I will be there soon."

Before anything else can be said, Maru pressed the end call button. Everyone in the room was silent, ingesting the information of a coming war to Earth. The fact of a coming alien invasion and that Maru was an alien are the only facts Will hid from the others. Though, he was sure the others had their suspicions about Maru being an alien.

Will stood and returned the phone to the man in the doorway.

"Just tell me one thing. What does CCU mean?" Will asked, confused, his voice back to normal.

"Creature Counter Unit. We are a secret organization created in the wake of an incident in Fresno a few months back. I'm sure you have seen the video of the chimera creatures, yes?" the man said.

"Yeah. I thought that was all an elaborate hoax, though."

"That is what we told the public. In reality, that was all real. We had to pay off a lot of people to keep it sounding like a hoax, too. It was to keep people from panicking over monsters being real. Looks like that may be a problem, now..."

"That's impossible. The combinations in those creatures are extreme. Almost impossible to exist together," Walt said, speaking for the first time, his face jiggling a little as he talked. He was a chubby man, but not as fat as when they were kids. He squinted his almond shaped eyes, probably recalling the creatures from that video with his photographic memory.

"They did, though. We examined the bodies. They were brought in by someone who was on the scene of that incident. They were functioning organisms. Now, can we please get going? My men are getting a little anxious. They would like to get back home."

"We're all going?" Will asked, surprised.

"Sorry, but you all know too much now-"

"Now we have to kill you?" Aaron chimed in, cautiously reaching behind his back, making a silent threat to the man.

"What? No. You kids watch too many movies. That stuff doesn't happen in real life. It's protocol."

The man turned his back to them and waved his other two men over. Like the man at the door, the other two men were dressed as civilians. But Will now knew that they were more than that, probably carrying weapons behind their backs, tucked in their pants, like Aaron. But unlike Aaron who had only a knife, the men probably had guns. Will suspected that if the 'friendly' encounter didn't go well, they would have resorted to their weapons. They were government agents after all.

"Are we ready to get going, finally?" the older, and biggest, of the two men asked.

"Yes. We are," the man by the door said.

"Finally," a younger man said.

They all three strode out, walking down the street. Maru didn't hesitate, following the three government agents. Will ran after Maru. Ashley followed Will. The others joined the group, curious and afraid of what was coming to Earth, thinking these men were their best chance of survival just as Will did.

8

Washington, D.C.

After a short walk to the men's SUV, and an even longer and crowded drive to Washington D.C., they arrived at the CCU headquarters in Buzzard Point, next to Ziegfeld's bar which was located on the peninsula that laid in confluence with the Pontiac River. The men that came to them introduced themselves to Will and his friends. The man with the Australian accent was Jake Walker. The older man, he looked to be about in his forties, was Damen Hlad. And the younger man, he looked to be in his late twenties or early thirties, was Alicio Brice. Walker pulled the SUV up to a five-story, red brick building. It looked like a newly built apartment or a hotel building. All ten of them, Maru included, piled out of the vehicle and into the building. The lobby of the building was an open space occupied by a single desk and elevators.

A hotel, Will concluded. *But why would this be the CCU HQ?*

They split up, piling into two different elevators. Will, Ashley, Maru, Walker, and Brice took the elevator up to the top floor, the doors opening into a long hallway lined with doors. Walker led them down the hallway to a door on the far end. They walked into a room filled with computer consoles and lots of people including the woman Will saw on the video chat. Another woman with big arm muscles and close cut blonde hair stood out in the room of computer technicians along with a skinny man in an expensive looking business suit and slicked back brown hair. The short haired woman introduced herself as Christina Angel.

"Ma'am," Walker said with a nod, sounding more like 'mom' with his accent to Will, making him chuckle.

She gave a nod back and said, "Great work, Walker."

"Where are our friends?" Will asked, looking back down the hallway they came down.

"They are being debriefed. You, Mr. William Carver, are the important one with your connection to Marugrah. We didn't want to upset you by separating you from your girlfriend so we had her come with you," the skinny man said, his hands behind his back.

Ashley's grip on Will's hand tightened. Something about this setup didn't sit well with her. He had to agree, as he felt the same way.

Marudon stepped out from behind Jessica's legs. Marugrah peeked out from around Will's legs, seeing her and ran toward her, embracing her in a weird reptilian hug. It made Will think maybe they had more of a relationship than just being protector and protected.

"And who are you?" Will asked, looking up from the reptilian hug fest.

"I am Lance Cole, Director of the Creature Containment Unit," the man said. "You know why the CCU was created, but it seems we will not be able to keep ourselves a secret for much longer. By this time tomorrow night, a monster will fall from the sky and land in New York City. A Vexnoxtuque is what Marudon has been calling it."

"A Kaiju," Will muttered.

"The size of the pod suggests it is as big, yes. Marudon says the creatures are unstoppable. Her army's laser fire only singed their armored skin. Our military's missiles and bullets will only explode harmlessly on the creatures. We are hopeless. But Marudon believes Marugrah can figure out a way to defeat the Kaijus inbound to our planet."

And what makes you people think I can defeat them? If I could, I wouldn't have fled my home world, Marugrah scoffed. He had already explained how he killed one on the video chat.

"Yes, I understand that. That device you mentioned, I think we have procured a few of them thanks to one of my agents."

What? That is impossible. That is Anterkian technology, hundreds of light years away from Earth and already conquered by the Plagueonians a very long time ago.

"But we do have a few. Ten in all. We kept them for study but we have reports that there were hundreds. Our agent, Ezekiel, was able to procure some after another encounter in Corfu, an island off Greece. They were attached to the heads of chimeras, like the ones from the video you all must have seen by now."

Impossible. That would mean the warmongers were here on Earth thousands of years ago, before human kind even existed.

Why would they be here then? Marudon asked, confusion in her telepathically projected voice.
I don't know but it's nothing good.

"So...what do we do then? Use those devices to control one of their monsters to use against them?" Will asked.

That is what I did on Anterkia. I failed, though. Other Vexnoxtuque overwhelmed the beast I controlled and destroyed it after I killed two. After that, it was a losing battle, Marugrah explained solemnly.

"How the hell are we supposed to do that?" Angel asked. "We going to attach the device to a rocket and fire it at the thing's head?"

"An excellent idea, squad leader," Cole said. "We should have something ready when the creature makes landfall."

"And what are we going to be doing in all this?" Will asked. "We're not soldiers. We have no military experience. We are of no use to you."

"On the contrary. You and your friends will be staying here for now, until this all blows over. We may need you come the time of the battle. And, I'm sure Marugrah would like you to stay."

Will glanced over at Maru, seeing his small friend nodding his agreement toward Cole's statement.

"What?" Ashley exclaimed. "I have work tomorrow. I can't just stay here."

"I'm sorry Ms. Singer, but we can't allow you to leave. You'll have to call in sick or something."

"But…"

"No buts. We *can't* allow you to leave," Angel growled, leveling a cold-eyed stare at Ashley that Will didn't like.

He didn't like the idea of staying in that place either as he had work in the next few days himself, but they were government agents and there was nothing they could do about it. They let themselves be ushered away by Walker. He led them, minus Marugrah who stayed with his Queen, back to the elevators which took them down one level. He opened a door two doors down from the elevators and waved them in. They walked in, surprising Will that the others were in the room. Will and Ashley walked into the room, the door shutting and locking behind them.

"Where'd you guys go?" Aaron asked, annoyed at their situation, standing beside the bed closest to the door.

"We were taken to some kind of control room on the floor above us," Will answered.

"Dude, for real. What the hell is going on? I am freaking out," Nicole said, slipping into a panic attack while sitting on a wooden chair. Jamie crouched from where he was standing, putting an arm around her, trying to calm her down

"Our situation is that there is an...alien monster on its way here, landing in New York City sometime tomorrow. A race of warmongering aliens are on their way after the monster to invade next with more monsters in their arsenal," Will explained.

"This is crazy, man. It's like something from a friggin' fifties science fiction movie!" Walt exclaimed, sitting on one of the three beds in the hotel room.

"I agree it is. This whole situation is fucked. If I hadn't seen it through Maru's eyes, I wouldn't have believed it myself. It's like something from a Godzilla movie... Just calm down, everyone."

"Will is right. Everyone just calm down. It all seems so surreal, I agree. But Maru is living proof of extraterrestrial existence. I mean, come on. A telepathically communicating, three-foot lizard. How is that not suspiciously alien?" Aaron said with a chuckle.

"You're right," Walt said, taking deep breaths and calming himself.

Nicole did the same.

Will walked over to the far bed, sitting down on it. Ashley joined him, sitting on the bed beside him.

"So... what are we supposed to do for fun?" Nicole asked, wiping tears from her eyes as Jamie rubbed her back.

Those two got a thing going on? Will wondered. He filed that thought away for later.

"Maybe this thing works?" Walt said, inspecting the television that sat in some kind of cabinet.

Ashley took her iPhone from her pocket, unlocking it. She tapped the screen bringing up the settings and tapping on the Wi-Fi settings.

"They have good Wi-Fi at least," she said.

Screaming filled the room, making everyone jump. Will looked up at the TV seeing Jason Voorhees chasing some girl in the woods. He let out a chuckle, everyone else following his lead. Their chuckles turned into laughter, easing away their tension of the situation they had found themselves in. After the laughter died down, Will laid back on the bed, exasperated with the day he had. Ashley appeared in his vision, looking down at him from above

"You alright there, cutie?" she asked.

"I'm just tired. This has been the craziest day of my life," Will replied, closing his eyes, mentally noting that she called him 'cutie'.

"Well none of us were expecting to be whisked away by government agents of a secret agency that fights monsters and aliens that wanna take over the universe," Aaron said.

"True dat," Jamie said.

Will felt Ashley cuddle up to him, her hand on his chest. He drifted off to sleep, listening to the sounds of the hockey masked killer cutting apart a teenage girl.

A knock on the door startled Will awake. He jumped up from the bed, accidently throwing Ashley off of him and waking up the rest of the room with her shout of surprise.

"Ow! What the hell, Will?" Ashley said, laying on the floor.

"I'm coming in!" an Australian accented voice said from behind the door that was knocked on.

Walker rushed in, waving a double barreled hand gun around the room and making everyone scream in fright. After Will finished screaming, he recognized the black gun Walker held in his hands. An AF2011-A1 double barrel semiautomatic pistol. It fired .45 rounds from a duplex single columned sixteen round clips (eight in each column) and was an extremely accurate weapon. Another one was holstered on his leg.

"I heard screaming," he said, confused.

"Yeah. It started when you knocked on the door and I woke up in a strange place," Will said, annoyed, helping Ashley off the floor and whispering 'sorry' over and over again to her.

"Ah, bloody hell. Of course," he said, putting his gun in the empty holster on his leg. That's when Will noticed the man's garb. He wore all black, some sort of tactical uniform with a Kevlar vest over his chest, a white 'CCU' stenciled on it. Full tactical gear. Ready for war.

"What time is it?" Aaron asked groggily.

"Seven in the morning," Walker said, looking at his watch.

"Holy shit, man," Nicole complained.

"Welcome to the military, missy," he mused.

"I didn't ask to, asshole," she hissed.

"Lazy buggers," he frowned.

Will cleared his throat, getting Walker's attention.

"You come here for a reason or did you just come to mess with us?" Will asked.

"Ah, yeah. Marugrah wanted to see you," Walker said.

Sup, female dogs, Maru said, suddenly on the bed beside Ashley, making her flinch in surprise.

"I think you mean 'bitches'," Jamie said with a grin.

They both mean the same thing, don't they?

"Yeah, they do. What's up, Maru?" Will asked.

I have spent all night helping these people create a missile pod device with the Anterkian telepathic unit. Just wanted to let you know that we are all ready to go. Cole is evacuating New York as we speak.

"How long 'till the Kaiju arrives?"

"Two hours," Walker spoke instead of Maru

"That's just great. Apocalypse incoming. Looks like we're going to die virgins, guys," Nicole joked.

"Who said we're all virgins?" Aaron asked.

"Not all of us are man whores, Aaron," Will laughed.

"You blokes are messed up in the head. There is a giant monster hurling toward Earth and you're making jokes," Walker said, walking out the door, annoyed with their banter.

"Mission accomplished. We made the soldier man uncomfortable," Jamie grinned.

"Screw you, mate," Walker yelled from the hallway.

"Sorry, I'm not into guys," Jamie yelled back.

"Alright, funny duddies," Walker said, walking back into the room, "let's go. Director Cole is waiting for you in the control room."

"Alright, we're coming Crocodile Dundee," Nicole said with a sly grin.

Walker mumbled something under his breath as he walked back into the hallway. Will and his friends filed out of the room. Walker waited for them by the elevator. They crammed into the elevator which took them up one level before opening and spilling them out into an identical hallway. Will and Ashley had been on this level before but the others had not. Walker led them down to the end of the hall, to a door on the right. They entered the dark room, the screens alive with footage of New York City from traffic cameras. People flooded through the streets, being escorted out of the city by military men and women. Military vehicles drove through the streets that were clear of any civilian vehicles, ready for the coming battle.

"Ah. Mr. Carver and company," Cole said, stepping out of the shadows of the room and into the lights pouring into the room from the hallway.

"Please, just call me Will," Will said.

"Okay, Will. As you can see, we are evacuating New York City. The military is moving into the city, as you can also see. The missile is en route now. It will be there within the hour. It will be fired from a FGM-148 Javelin rocket launcher into the creature's neck. We have more missiles being developed as well in hopes to turn the Plagueonians' weapons against them."

It is a good plan. A smart plan. I don't give you humans enough credit, Marugrah said, his scary reptilian teeth showing.

"When's the show start?" Walt asked, talking for the first time this morning. He wasn't much of a talker anyways, Will knew.

"Approximately two hours until the pod lands. We estimate it will land in Central Park. Our troops are positioning themselves around it," Angel said, her form outlined by the glow of the screens.

"Well...let's try to stop the apocalypse, eh?" Will said,

55

finding Ashley's hand for comfort.

56

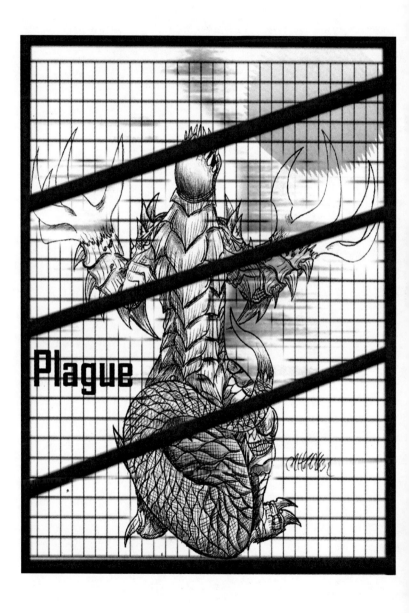

9

New York City

New York City, normally having a population of eight million people, was now only populated by the hundreds of military soldiers surrounding Central Park where the monster from the stars was supposed to land. Central Park was an urban park opened in 1856 on 778 acres of city owned land in middle-upper Manhattan. It was the most visited spot in the United States. On any other occasion, it would have been a beautiful place to hang out, but sergeant Nick Huber knew this was no ordinary day. Today was the *supposed* beginning of the apocalypse.

He walked over to the man holding the Javelin, Private Jake Doland, who was watching the sky from their position on 59th street on the south side of the park. Everyone was skeptical about this whole idea. They were only going on information from a new agency created in the last few months. Kind of shady if you asked him. None of them had heard of the Creature Containment Unit before now. None of them believed in this whole mess going on but the higher ups did. They were supposedly presented with proof upon the danger of the situation and his job was not to question orders given to him but to follow them.

I guess we will find out soon whether this shit is real, Huber thought, still skeptical. He watched the white fluffy clouds pass overhead through the bright blue sky.

"You really think it's coming, sir?" Doland asked.

"I'm not sure, private. The CCU jerk-wads seem to think it is, though," Huber replied. "And our job is not to question orders."

"Yeah. I guess we will find out soon enough, huh? It's almost the time they predicted the creature will land," Doland said, mirroring Huber's earlier assessment as he looked at his tactical watch.

A thunderous crackling filled the air, followed by the sky lighting up blindingly bright. A flaming cylindrical object rocketed from the sky, landing in the Jacqueline Kennedy Onassis Reservoir, a 106 acres across and 29-foot-deep body of water located closer to the north end of the park but was mostly in the middle. Water and earth exploded into the air, most of the water turning to steam from contact with the burning hot object. The shock wave from the object landing uprooted trees and flung them away from the reservoir and thrown to the ground, giving Huber's team a better look at the destruction wrought. A few trees were flung over his and his team's head, making them drop to the ground. When the men got back to their feet, they readied their guns, including Doland. He put a hand on Doland's shoulder, calming the man. The rocket contained within his Javelin was something cooked up by the CCU. Some kind of mind control device, they said. He had no idea if something like that would control a beast the size of the metal cylinder before him was.

The steam dissipated into the air, giving Huber a clear look at the pod laying in the now empty reservoir. Most of the trees in the park were now overturned and flattened to the ground, unable to obscure any of the military teams' view surrounding the park of what happened next. The pod split down the middle, the two sides flinging away, revealing something so terrifying, it made Huber stumble back a few steps. The head of the creature that emerged from the pod looked like it was a flaming skull. It wasn't a human skull, however. The top of the skull was a half circle piece of bone curving down to jagged, sharp teeth. The creature's jaw was the same, but thinner and more of an oval than a circle. It lacked any eyes or eye sockets that he could see. Its back was lined with spiked plates of overlapping armor, ending at the base of the creature's tail. White armor plates ran down from the creature's neck down to its crotch. Its arms were armored, jagged spikes rising out of the monster's shoulders. Three spikes poked out of the creature's armored forearms. The hands looked as if they burned red-hot, the black skin of its wrists looking as if they were melted away, the four digits at the end twitching with energy. A gigantic spike protruded from each of its elbows. Its sides rippled with weirdly arranged muscles which continued throughout the monster's tail that ended in burning flames. The skin at the end of the tail also looking as if it were melted away. Bone white armor ran down the front of its legs, ending at its kneecap. Its leg muscles were also chaotically arranged, its four toes looking like skeletal digits tipped with deadly claws. Spikes protruded from its calf.

The Kaiju (that was the term the CCU was using for the monster) let out a deafening roar, making the men cringe and want to cover their ears. Huber figured it was probably heard for miles all around. The men's faces around him twisted with terror, but they stood their ground, guns at the ready and pointed at the Kaiju hovering four-hundred-feet over the park. The Kaiju lifted itself out of the cratered pond with one of its massive legs which decimated one half of the Metropolitan Museum of Art as it landed. Once clear of the pond, four Sikorsky UH-60 Black Hawk attack helicopters descended from the sky, raining down AGM-114 Hellfire laser guided missiles, 70 mm Hydra rockets, and AIM-92 Stinger air-to-air missiles upon the horrifying monstrosity. Huber was surprised that the beast didn't even flinch at -or even notice- the missiles bombarding its body while standing in the Great Lawn, the almost flat site of the thirty-five-acre lower reservoir. He was briefed that the creatures would withstand them, but it seemed impossible to him. He had seen the damage the missiles can do first hand, as he was sometimes the one firing them. But here he was, watching the impossible.

The helicopters started swinging around, trying to get the Kaiju to turn its back to Huber's team so they can fire the device at the back of its neck. The creature tracked the choppers with its head, somehow seeing them with no eyes, following the annoying buzzing machines as they formed a line, backing away. The Kaiju followed their lead, turning its body when it could no longer track them with its head. When the monster's back was to them, Huber tapped Doland on the shoulder. He knew what to do. He put his eye up to the eye piece, targeting the back of the creature's neck. Once locked on, he pulled the trigger. The rocket erupted from the launcher with a hiss, rocketing away toward its target.

It slammed into the creature's armored neck, between a plate of armor and the back of the Kaiju's flaming head where the monster's spine should be, the casing splitting apart and flying away upon impact.

Huber toggled his throat mic, "Come in command. This is Alpha team. Objective complete."

"Roger that Alpha team," a woman's voice said through the mic. "Command out."

Huber looked up as the monster opened its mouth wide, letting loose a torrent of flames which struck the Black Hawk in the front of the line. The flame must've ignited the chopper's fuel because it erupted into a ball of fire, plummeting to the ground and landing in a pile of uprooted trees, setting them on fire as well.

"Holy shit!" Doland exclaimed, reeling back in fright.

"What do we do now?" another man in Huber's team, who he knew as Lyngly, asked.

"Nothing. Our objective is complete. It's up to Beta Team now," Huber said. "We wait for further orders."

The Black Hawks spread out, forming a horizontal line and unleashing gatling gunfire upon the Kaiju. Two A-10 Thunderbolts, also known as Warthogs, passed overhead, raining down AIM-9 Sidewinder air-to-air missiles and AGM-65 Maverick missiles down on the monster's back, careful not to hit the back of its neck where the black box resided. The monster roared angrily up at the jets as they passed over it. It lifted one of its massive legs, about to take a step but froze. It shook its head back and forth like a wet dog shaking off water. But Huber knew that wasn't what the Kaiju was doing. It threw its head back, letting out a high pitched wail before grabbing its head with its massive fiery hands. The chain gunfire stopped.

The device is working, Huber realized. *They're getting*

inside its head!

The creature cradled its head, hunching over. Huber felt hopeful that they would able to stop this monster with a relatively small loss of life. The four men aboard the Black Hawk that erupted in flames are most definitely dead.

It lasted only a few moments before it all drained away.

The monster pulled its hands away from its head and stood up straight. It roared in what looked to Huber like victory. It lashed a hand out, striking a Black Hawk that was foolishly close. Huber watched in horror as the helicopter plummeted to the ground where it was crushed under the giant's foot. The two remaining Black Hawks opened fire with their gatling guns once again, further annoying the behemoth. It let loose with a torrent of fire from its mouth, destroying another Black Hawk.

Perhaps in an attempt to save the remaining helicopter, three M1A2 Abrams main battle tanks rolled into the park from the north side, crushing tree branches beneath their treads as they weaved their way inside while firing 120 mm rounds at the Kaiju's chest. The monster looked down at the small annoyances with rage. It did, in fact, allow the Black Hawk to escape safely. The Kaiju walked around the reservoir, stomping its way toward the tanks firing at it.

And Beta Team.

That was when the A-10 Thunderbolts returned, firing more Sidewinders and Mavericks at the beast, getting a cheer out of Huber's men. But the missiles just made the beast angrier. It jumped up, the ground and uprooted trees crumbling beneath its feet, mouth agape. It caught one of the Thunderbolts in its massive maw, seemingly swallowing the plane whole. The earth was decimated as the creature's massive weight slammed back into it. It spat out the plane, hacking it at the three battle tanks who tried to move out of the way but weren't able to move fast enough. Two of the three tanks were crushed beneath the lougied jet.

The remaining tank made its way back out of the park through the mess of trees and slipped in between the buildings fringing the north side of the park. The Kaiju let out an angry growl as it charged toward the buildings.

"That thing is going to decimate Beta squad!" Doland yelled.

"Command to all ground teams. Fire everything you have at the Kaiju. Aim for its legs. Maybe you can cripple it," the woman who served as command's voice came through Huber's ear piece.

"Affirmative," he said into his mic, turning toward his men while hefting up a M32 rotary grenade launcher. "You heard the lady! Move! We need to help them!"

Huber weaved his way around uprooted trees, past the Lake, across the decimated Great Lawn, past the reservoir, all the way to the north end as the Kaiju decimated the buildings fringing it. Huber and his men were exhausted once they reached it, having run the length of the 843-acre land as fast as they could. They all carried heavy hitting weapons, rocket launchers and grenade launchers as well, not making the run any easier.

They raised their weapons, firing them at the creature's armored back and legs as it swung its massive hands back and forth, decimating stone and melting metal, pushing its way into the street the tank was retreating down. The monster was a half mile into the city from the park when Huber's team started firing. The monster continued its rage filled rampage before noticing the rockets and grenades peppering its back and legs. It whirled around, sighting in on the five men launching artillery at it. It let out an ear splitting roar, making the men cringe.

Huber gasped in horror as flames erupted from the monster's gullet, washing over the five men. They didn't even have time to scream before they ceased to exist, their bodies turned to ash.

10

Washington, D.C.

Marugrah watched the big screen in the front of the control room that showed satellite footage of Central Park. Men gathered on the north and south sides. A flash of light momentarily obscured their vision before a fiery object landed in the reservoir. After a few moments, the pod split apart, revealing the Vexnoxtuque, the Kaiju, the Plagueonians sent as their harbinger. He couldn't tell what species it was before the Plagueonians experimented upon it. He watched the Kaiju stepped out of the empty reservoir and onto the Great Lawn, helicopters swooping around it, firing missiles at it. It turned its back to Alpha Team, allowing them to fire the device at the back of the creature's head.

Marugrah adjusted the black metal headband on his head. The head band would allow him to access the Kaiju's mind and battle it for control over its body. Once he won, he would be able to control the monster's body and use it against its makers. He had only done it once before. It was difficult, but he believed he could get it done. Depending on the species...

"Come in command. This is Alpha Team. Objective complete," a man's voice said, the screen identifying the speaker as sergeant Nick Huber along with background information about the man.

"Copy that, Alpha Team. Command out," Angel said, turning to Marugrah. "Your time to shine."

Marugrah looked around the room at the people standing in it, from Marudon, his Queen, to Will, a human he could actually call his friend even with their...strained relationship. Will gave him a smile and a nod, boosting his confidence level a little more. He activated the device mentally, connecting him to the Kaiju's mind.

He slipped out of his mind and into the Kaiju's, feeling the creature's rage and blood lust toward humanity. He came face to ugly face with the monster, which looked oddly familiar to him but at the same time not.

"Who are you?" the creature asked, its skull-like mouth not moving as it spoke and tilted to the side.

"I am Marugrah, guardian of the Queen of...," he started.

"Maruia. You are a Maruian?"

Marugrah's eyes widened as a sensation enveloped

him. A familiar sensation of a killer. Of a destroyer of worlds. Of his world.

The creature before him was a Plagueonian.

"Who are you," Marugrah asked.

"I am Plague, prince of Plagueonia. Destroyer of worlds. Like yours, Maruian," the creature known as Plague said. The creature's appearance shifted from the monster in New York to a more familiar form. His head looked vaguely humanoid, standing like a human on two armored back legs. But the armor wasn't like the armor on his Kaiju form. It was silver with symbols carved into it. He wore the same armor all over his body, a red cape fluttering behind him. A curved helmet sat atop his head, framing his black eyes, flat nose, and wicked, sharp-toothed smile. "Maybe you'd recognize me better like this."

"I recognize you just by your name, monster. It's impossible that you're alive. You died. I killed you myself."

"Yes, I remember that. The alterations to my body were the only way to save my life. By becoming one of our repulsive Vexnoxtuque, I was granted regenerative abilities that saved my life. It is disgusting but it has allowed me to continue conquering worlds like this ball of dirt I am on now," Plague said.

"I won't allow you to conquer this planet."

Plague let out a cackle. "You think you can take over my mind? I saw you do that on Anterkia. You're not doing that this time. Goodbye, Maruian."

With a wave of Plague's four-digit hand, Marugrah was thrown out of Plague's mind violently. He grabbed his head, letting out a high pitched squeal of pain. His brain felt like it was on fire, soon fading away to a dull headache.

"Maru!" he heard Will yell as his mind slipped from New York to his body in Washington D.C., making him open his eyes. Will, Ashley, Aaron, Nicole, Jamie, Walt, Marudon, and Angel stood over him, as he laid on his back on the carpeted floor of the control room.

"Are you in control?" Angel asked as he stood up from the floor.

If I were in control, I would still be laying on the floor, Marugrah snapped.

"What happened?" Will asked.

What happened was that thing in New York is a Plagueonian I thought I killed a long time ago. I was wrong, it seems. He was saved by being turned into a Vexnoxtuque.

Marudon looked stunned, probably realizing who he was talking about. *You don't mean...*

Yes. Plague.

"Sounds like a Batman villain's name," Aaron retorted.

He is indeed a villain, but not of Batman's. Of the galaxy's. And mine. Plague was the prince of the Plagueonian race, son of the Plagueonian Queen. I thought I killed him at the battle for Anterkia. However, he must have been recovered and saved by being turned into the monster you see on the screen, Marugrah explained, turning toward the big screen displaying the satellite footage of New York. Plague jumped into the sky, snatching a jet in his jaws and falling back to the ground. He then spat the jet out at the tanks that entered the park, destroying two of them.

"So that is their harbinger... One of their own," Cole said, stepping into the glow of the screen from the shadows, watching Plague's rampage, seeming a little too interested in the revelation.

It would seem so, yes, Marugrah said, a little bit annoyed at his interest.

"What the hell are we supposed to do about it now? You guys got a spare giant robot around we can use to fight it?" Nicole asked sarcastically.

"That would be awesome," Jamie whispered, but Maru heard it perfectly.

"No, we don't have a giant robot, as convenient as that would be. All we can really do is throw everything we have in our arsenal at it, hoping to injure it or slow it down," Cole said solemnly.

"Even nuclear options?" Evangeline asked, shocked.

"If it comes to it, yes."

Marugrah looked up to see Will cringe at the words. He searched Will's mind, finding information on atomic bombs and nuclear weaponry, seeing their destructive power. They might be enough to kill Plague but at the cost of New York City...and any of the military troops in the city.

"Command to all ground teams. Fire everything you have at the Kaiju. Aim for its legs. Maybe you can cripple it," Angel said into her headset. Maru heard the doubt in her last sentence. She didn't believe they could really cripple it. And neither did Maru.

Affirmatives came in through the screen. Marugrah looked to the screen, seeing Plague making his way into the city as he followed the soldiers retreating into the city. The squad of soldiers that were responsible for firing the black box device at Plague were running through the park toward the monster. Once they reached him, they fired their weapons at him only to be doused with fire and turned into piles of ash and melted metal.

"This is a losing battle," Walt said, a defeated look on his face.

Marugrah knew he was right. There was no known way to kill a Vexnoxtuque without another Vexnoxtuque to fight and kill it and they didn't have one, let alone the technology to make one of their own. And he was desperate enough to do just that, no matter how disgusting of a thought it was. It was the only way to stop the giant creatures. A plan started formulating in his mind, but it would only work when the Plagueonians arrived. And even then it might be too late.

"I'm gonna be sick," Ashley groaned, burying her face in Will's chest. He put his arms around her, doing his best to comfort her. He ushered her out of the room and out of Marugrah's sight.

What are you thinking? Marudon asked, keeping her voice limited to Marugrah's mind.

I'm thinking that he is right. This is a losing battle. We have no way of stopping Plague or any of the other Vexnoxtuque in their arsenal, Marugrah replied, masking his real thoughts.

You may be right but we still have a few more Anterkian neural interface boxes. If another Vexnoxtuque falls from the sky, we can take control of it. We could but we aren't guaranteed access. Like me with Plague, we could be thrown out of their heads. Not to mention, Plague could decimate a few cities before then as well.

Frantic chatter flooded from the screen into Marugrah's ears. They were losing horribly against the monster devastating the city.

Burned alive.

Crushed within their war machines or under Plague's colossal feet.

Dying.

"Half of our ground troops have been annihilated. More air support is inbound," a man at a console reported.

"Shit. Half? How many troops did you guys send out there?" Aaron asked, astonished.

"We sent four hundred, including the men in the helicopters and tanks," Cole replied.

"So, this monster, Plague, has killed two hundred people so far, that quickly?"

"Yeah... And the number is climbing. Anyone that gets in its way are killed. We may want to review our remaining options." He nodded to Angel who knew what he was implying.

Remaining options? Marugrah asked, watching Angel walk away, pulling out a phone. *You're talking about nuclear weapons.*

"Something of the same power, yes. It may be the only way we can stop the Kaiju."

At the cost of your own city!

"It is a price we have to pay for the sake of humanity."

Is that what you plan on doing with every Vexnoxtuque that falls from the sky? Drop an atomic bomb on it?

"If it kills them and saves us from being eradicated, I will do what I think is necessary."

You're a fool, Cole.

"A fool with no other options and is looking out for his species. At least I am fighting for my planet instead of fleeing it and bringing that trouble on another world."

Cole gave Marugrah a stern look, sparking his anger. He started growling, hooking his claws and about to attack the man but was stopped by Marudon's hand on his scaly shoulder. He looked into her green eyes, calming himself in them. Cole gave him a squinty eyed look before turning back to the screen, hands behind his back.

Marugrah was seeing a new side to the man. A cold side. But it didn't mean Cole wasn't right. Marugrah ran as his home world was ravaged. If he would have stayed, they might have stood a chance of stopping the Plagueonians on Maruia and Earth would have been spared from the destruction now being wrought. They were only here because Marugrah and Marudon were. Or were they?

"Everything is under way, sir. A bomber will be there within the hour," Angel said, walking back in the room.

"Good. Let's hope it works. We'll hit it with MOABs before we resort to the nuclear option, Maru," Cole said. "I know you are not familiar with the weapon. MOAB stands for Massive Ordinance Air Blast. The largest *non-nuclear* weapon in the U.S. arsenal. It's a vacuum bomb equivalent to eleven tons of TNT that basically melts everything within a one-mile radius. It's a fuel-air explosive, meaning it will detonate before hitting its target, creating a thermobaric wave of force and heat. It is close to a nuke in power."

Aaron let out a disgusted sigh as he made his way out

of the control room, Walt, Jamie, and Nicole following him. Marugrah took one last look at Cole's cold eyes before following them out, Marudon on his short tail.

"Can you believe this shit?" Aaron asked as they walked into the hallway.

"You mean, sacrificing New York City to stop an unstoppable monster? I mean, the city has been evacuated. And they'll pull the remaining soldiers out of the city. It'll just be the monster and buildings. I don't like it any more than anyone else but if they can kill the Kaiju, then why stop them? We have who-knows-how-many-more on the way," Will said, disgust mixed with determination on his face.

"He's right," Ashley agreed. "New York can be rebuilt."

The destruction isn't going to be just limited to New York, either, Marugrah chimed in.

"The whole world could be destroyed if they don't at least try to stop Plague," Walt said.

"Do we at least agree that it makes us all sick to our stomachs?" Aaron asked.

Everyone nodded their heads.

"Good."

11

New York

Jason Keen flew the B-2 Spirit stealth bomber toward the target, the city of New York racing toward him in his windshield. He looked to his right where his co-pilot, and mission commander, Cody Stewart, sat, giving him a nod as they approached the Kaiju code-named 'Plague' carving a path of destruction through the theater district from the now demolished Central Park as it pushed its way south, heading who-knows-where. After ridding the north side of soldiers the monster headed back through Central Park to the south side. It looked to Keen that it was heading down the coast.

Toward Washington D.C.

If the creature was smart enough, it could have slipped into the waterways surrounding New York and make its way along the coast from there. Maybe it just liked to cause destruction? Maybe it was afraid of water? Or maybe it really was just dumb.

Keen didn't know anything about the monster or what it wanted, and didn't care. His only job was to drop a MOAB on its ugly flaming head, erasing it from existence. He flicked a switch, opening the bay doors on the bottom of the triangular craft. Another flick of a switch released the MOAB. The MOAB fell from the bomber's belly, landing on the monster's head and detonating with a powerful force. Keen didn't feel any of its effects as he was tens of thousands of feet above the ground when it detonated.

He guided the bomber around in a half circle, coming around for a look. A mile-wide radius around where the MOAB was dropped was smoldering ash. Buildings laid in blackened ruins. The air burnt. No sign of Plague, though. It was like the creature was vaporized by the bomb.

Then, the blackened husks of toppled buildings

shifted, and parted as the monster rose from under them, unharmed. It seemingly roared up at him, looking very pissed off and probably sounded the same way. Keen was too far up for the monster to reach him, so he wasn't too worried. A big gray blur sped past his craft, startling him.

"What the hell was that?" Stewart asked.

"No idea. All I saw was a blur," Keen said.

Keen circled around, looking for the object. He didn't see anything...until he did. He couldn't believe what he was looking at. He was looking at what seemed to be a flying saucer. A disk spun around a circular grey orb with alien carvings all over it.

"What in God's name is that?" Stewart asked.

"It looks like a UFO," Keen said, flying around the object.

The object seemed to spot them, a red dot on the grey orb's hull sighting in on the bomber. Keen pulled away from the object, the radar showing it on his ass.

"Shit! It's following us!" Stewart yelled.

"I can see that," Keen growled, pushing the bomber to its top speed of 630 miles per hour. He tried to shake it off using evasive maneuvers, but the thing kept up. The craft shuddered from an impact as alarms rang throughout the craft. They had been hit.

But hit by what?

A missile?

A bullet?

What did the thing chasing them even use as a weapon?

Keen had a million questions about the object following them but he didn't think anyone could answer

77

them. Or that he'd survive to ask them.

A second impact rocked the bomber. He checked the displays seeing the thrusters were damaged and failing. They were going down.

He fought with the controls, losing an already lost battle. Stewart screamed as the view out the windshield changed from blue sky to tall grey buildings. Keen frantically fought to pull the craft up when they suddenly stopped in midair, three hundred and fifty feet from the ground.

They were spun around, Keen catching a glimpse of massive burning digits before coming face-to-face with the flaming skulled monster Plague. Stewart squealed in fright, Keen joining him.

The Kaiju opened its massive maw, letting loose a loud roar that made the men quit their screaming and cover their ears. When they pulled their hands away, they were covered in blood. The creature's roar had burst their eardrums so they weren't able to hear the order to eject from command.

Plague watched them quiver in fear before opening his mouth again and letting loose a stream of fire upon the craft which exploded in the Kaiju's already burning hands.

12

Washington, D.C.

"Are you shitting me? It shrugged off the Mother Of All

Bombs and destroyed the bomber?" Angel asked, shocked at the event that transpired in just minutes.

"It had help. Zoom in on that object above the creature," Cole said, pointing to an aberration on the feed.

Just as Cole commanded, the screen zoomed in on the object hovering just a hundred feet above Plague, making Will gasp. The object was a grey sphere with a ring of metal spinning around it. A red circle was the only blemish on the symbol covered hull's smooth surface.

"Is that...?" Ashley started, but never finished her sentence.

"A UFO... A flying saucer," Will said in awe. It looked a lot like alien nut jobs spot all the time, but he doubted that they saw this exact same craft. Probably crafts of similar design, though.

Not just any flying saucer. A Plagueonian research vessel. It monitors the Vexnoxtuque's vitals and provides it with energy if it cannot find a food source. We need to seize that vessel, Marugrah said, looking a little more excited than he should.

"Why not just blow it up?" Cole asked, turning his attention away from the screen and toward the three-foot-tall alien lizard-dragon.

You saw how ineffective your MOAB was on the Vexnoxtuque, you will have no further luck with the orb. It has a high grade shield protecting it, not to mention it will shoot anything that approaches it or Plague now that it has arrived.

"So, what? You want me to drop a team on the thing, infiltrate it, and disable its shields?"

No. Just me.

"Why would I do that?"

Because I am the only one that can fly my ship which has cloaking capabilities. That is the only thing that will be able to get even remotely close to that vessel. Like I said, anything else will be shot from the sky. Anything they can see, at least.

Will watched in horror as Cole considered the idea. The plan was dangerous and he suspected Marugrah had an ulterior motive for entering that ship. What it was, he had no idea. Revenge, maybe.

"You make a convincing case, Marugrah," Cole said. "Sergeant Hlad will escort you to your ship."

The big man stepped forward, running a giant hand through the short white hair atop his head.

"Maru, are you sure about this?" Will asked him.

It may be the only way to stop Plague, Marugrah told him.

Will looked into the alien lizard's reptilian eyes, seeing nothing but the truth in them. Marugrah gave him his best smile since he lacked the face muscles to make a human-like smile. He gave Marugrah a smile of his own, approving of the mission. If he had a way to stop Plague, they had to try it. He didn't want to see his planet and everyone he loved fall to the alien invaders.

"Fine, fine," Will said. "If it will stop Plague, we'll try it."

Marugrah nodded and followed the giant of a man out of the control room. Will thought on it a moment before following them to the elevator at the end of the hallway. They took the elevator down, the door opening up into a basement. Hlad flipped a switch revealing a big object sitting in the middle of the room, covered with a black tarp. Hlad walked over to the object and pulled the tarp off of it, revealing a gold oval shaped craft covered in alien symbols. The symbols are way different than the ones on the Plagueonian craft, though. Less...sinister.

Marugrah bounced over to it, running his hands across the shiny hull. Will laughed as Maru seemingly hugged the ship. Maru gave him a squinty eyed look, shutting him up. Maru tapped a section near the middle of the side of the ship. A panel appeared and Maru typed in a code. The door swung upwards, revealing its insides which was nothing more than a silver space with a rack that looked to adorn some kind of gun.

"I believe you will find everything is in working order," Hlad said.

Maru climbed inside the small ship, moving out of sight. Beeping came from the inside of the ship as Will watched the hatch. He didn't know what Maru was doing in there but he figured he was checking out the ship's vitals.

You are correct. Everything is in working order, Maru said, returning to Will's view and hopping out of the ship.

"Good. We didn't touch the craft after we brought it here. Marudon took some stuff out of some crates that were in here but that was about it," Hlad explained.

The devices she made?

"Yeah. She made them from stuff aboard the ship."

Alright, how do I fly this out of here?

Hlad hit a button next to the light switch. A hatch at the far end of the basement opened.

Ah. That's how, Maru said, climbing back into the

ship.

"Wait, you're going by yourself?" Will asked.

Of course I am.

"Let me go with you."

No, Will. This task is very dangerous and I don't want to see you hurt or worse...dead. Ashley would be very displeased with me if that happened.

"I know the risks involved and I don't care. I want to help. I'm not going to just sit idly by while the world goes to shit. If there is something I can do, I want to do it."

I admire your enthusiasm about fighting the invading force but this isn't a job for a human.

"Too bad. I'm coming with you."

Before Maru could protest, Will slid into the small craft obviously built for three-foot-tall alien lizards. The craft was maybe five feet tall and ten feet long. Maru gave him an angry look before heading toward the cockpit with what Will could only guess was a exasperated gasp.

"Wait a second," Hlad said, walking toward the ship. He took off his Kevlar vest, removing a gun from the holster attached to the vest's chest, and handed it to Will. "Take it."

Will took the vest and put it on the best he could in the small space for his six foot hight.

"This too," Hlad said, second guessing the decision to remove the hand gun and handed him the 9mm M9 Baretta and two spare magazines.

Will took the gun hesitantly, sliding it back in the holster attached to the vest on his chest.

The gun must have some sentimental value to the man,

Will thought.

It's not like it'll do any good, Marugrah scoffed.

"It'll have to do. Thanks, sergeant," Will said.

Hlad nodded and closed the hatch. Maru lifted the ship off the ground and out of the hatch. Will shuffled toward the cockpit, hunched over as he couldn't stand up fully in the ship. He watched as they ascended into the sky and speeded toward New York at Mach 3, the fastest they could safely go through without killing themselves.

"Are we cloaked?" Will asked.

Yep. We cloaked before I even exited the CCU building, Marugrah said.

"How long until we reach New York?"

About ten minutes.

"Awesome."

We are heading toward one of thousands of ships of the invaders and destroyers of Earth as well as one of their ultimate weapons. How is any of that awesome?

"Sarcasm, dude. I don't find this scenario awesome at all."

Oh. I haven't quite mastered reading human seriousness or sarcasticness yet.

"So, I've noticed."

They spent the ride to New York City in silence. Plague was almost out of the city, heading south through China Town, back the way Will and Maru had just came from.

Where the hell is it going? Will wondered.

His task is to eliminate this country's leader, Marugrah answered, answering Will's mental question.

"So its headed for D.C. That is an even better reason to stop it here and now," Will said. His friends were

there and he'd be damned if he let this creature go there
and put them in danger as it rampaged toward the White
House to kill the President.

Agreed.

Marugrah guided the ship to the miniature grey
Saturn-like craft hovering over the Kaiju charging
through the city. Will almost expected a laser bolt to
shoot out of the red eye adorning the smooth gray
surface of the sphere like it did with the B2 bomber but
none came. It seemed the cloaking covering the ship was
doing its job. Thankfully. He wasn't too fond of being
blown up.

Maru gently docked the ship to the top of the grey
sphere, careful not to alert them to their presence. He
hopped from his seat behind the controls and made a
shooing motion with his small clawed hands, making
Will scoot to the back of the cargo bay. Maru came in,
putting a hand on the ship's floor. A light traced a
rectangular section on the floor and lifted up, revealing
the shiny grey, symbol covered hull of the Plagueonian
ship beneath. He put his hand on the grey surface,
opening another hatch that revealed a glowing gold
walkway beyond it.

Hand me that gun over there, Maru said, pointing at
the rack beside Will.

Will plucked the small gun and handed it to Maru who
took the weapon, jumping through the hatch in the floor.
Will dropped through the hatch next, drawing the
Baretta from the chest holster on his vest, holding it like
his dad taught him to when they used to hunt together
when he was a kid. The walkway they landed on was a
mix of gold and grey coloring that looked to run the top

circumference of the sphere.

"Okay, where to now, boss?" Will asked with a smirk, sweeping the eight and a half-foot tall and six-foot-wide hallway.

Just follow me, Maru said, annoyed as he swept his gun in the same manner.

Maru led Will down the hallway, coming upon a door. He put his hand on the door which slid into the wall revealing a grey space that looked like an elevator.

"What's this?" Will asked.

A lift that will take us to the center of the ship, where we need to be, Maru vaguely explained.

Maru stepped onto the lift, Will following suit. They rode the lift down for a minute before it stopped and the lift door slid open. As the door opened, Maru fired a shot, hitting an eight-foot armored creature in the head. Will didn't get a good look at the creature before Maru blasted its head off. They stepped out of the lift tube and into what looked like a laboratory, sweeping the area with their weapons.

Hit that red button on the side of the lift, Maru said, pointing his gun at the cowering grey giants that littered the hundred-foot-diameter space.

Will complied, hitting the button with a closed fist, staying near the lift. He shifted his gaze to the creatures in the room. They wore some sort of weird looking white clothing. They had bald, circular heads with wide human-like pure black eyes. Their noses were nothing more than two thin slits and their mouths were just lipless lines stretched into a frown of horror with razor sharp teeth. He couldn't see the creature's body but he knew they were probably very powerful. Or not for these guys. Their arms looked about as thick as a human arm, ending in four sharp digits. Will didn't see any claws but knew they could eviscerate him with one swipe. Their legs were equally thick with more dog-like legs ending in four digits on their feet. They didn't look like soldiers but more like scientists.

Will found it a bit humorous that the so called 'warmongers' were afraid of just two creatures smaller than them. There were at least twenty Plagueonians in the lab. They could easily overtake Maru and Will but instead they cowered in fear of them.

Definitely scientists.

As for the room, it looked to span the whole circumference of the middle of the orb. It was full of lab tables, monitors, and scary looking devices hanging from the ceiling ten-feet above them.

Who is the head scientist? Maru asked, forcefully thrusting his gun toward the crowd of cowering creatures.

A Plagueonian with an intricately designed cloak stepped forward.

"I am," the creature said, its voice deep and menacing but was scared out of its mind.

Prep a table, Maru demanded, training his gun on the creature.

"What? Are you crazy? These stations are for creating Vexnoxtuque," the Plagueonian said, horror written all over his face.

"Maru, what the hell? I thought we were stopping Plague by blowing the shit out of this place," Will said, just as horrified as the Plagueonian.

I'm sorry, Will. I lied to Cole. The only way to stop

Plague is to become what he is, Marugrah said, head down in shame for lying.

Will ground his teeth together in frustration. He didn't want to lose his friend but he didn't want to lose the world either. Or his friends in D.C. with which the rampaging monster beneath them was heading toward. Maru looked at him, seeing his frustration. Maru's eyes were full of sorrow at his friend's pain.

"Fine, do it," Will said, turning away from Maru.

He turned back to see Maru jumping up on one of the tables, gun still in his hand. Some of the Plagueonians were relaxing until he brought up his own gun, and they tensed up again. The head scientist brought down an injector looking tool that was hanging from the ceiling and plunged the needle into Maru's arm, depressing the trigger. Green fluid surged through the cord attached to the room's ceiling, through the futuristic looking injector gun and into Marugrah.

His body seized as the fluid entered his body, doing who-knows-what to his physiology. Well, Will did know what was happening to him. He was being turned into a Kaiju. A Vexnoxtuque. Could he fight whatever the Plagueonians used to control the giant creatures? Did they even use anything to control the giants? Will had no idea how that worked.

Will...get out of here. Take the ship and go back to D.C., Maru said, looking a little woozy.

"How the hell am I supposed to fly it out of here? I know nothing of flying a space ship," Will said, confused, not wanting to leave his friend.

It will adjust itself to accommodate any life form in the driver's seat, Maru explained, grinding his teeth in obvious pain. Whatever was injected into him was working its way through his body and it hurt a lot. *Now go!*

Will turned to the lift, putting a hand on the lift's door but nothing happened.

"You have to release the lift lock," one of the Plagueonians said, confusing him as to why it would help him.

Will ignored his confusion and hit the red button on the side of the tubular structure that was the lift, the door immediately opening. He jumped to the side as three armed Plagueonians in silver armor and some sort of black fibered under suit rushed out of the lift, their weapons pointed at Maru. Will pushed himself against the side of the lift tube, peeking around at the action. Spikes seemingly exploded from the skin on Maru's head, knees, elbow, the end of his tail and the sides of his back. His muscles rippled unnaturally under his scaly skin. And he was a good foot taller.

While the Plagueonian soldiers were busy watching Maru's transformation in horror, Will slipped around the lift's circumference and into the lift opening. The lift door closed as Maru let out a scary, foreboding roar that was unlike anything Will had ever heard from the alien lizard before. His stomach lurched as the lift ascended, opening at the walkway they first arrived at. He walked the way they came, finding the opening they jumped down from...and a Plagueonian soldier looking up at it, weapon raised.

He raised his own weapon, aiming at the creature's helmeted head. He squeezed the trigger, firing off three shots that just ricocheted off its helmet. The Plagueonian turned toward him, probably pissed off. It was hard to tell with the alien's eyes being behind a black visor. But by the way it bared its teeth, Will could tell it was pretty mad. It raised its weapon, a futuristic looking rifle not unlike Maru's, toward him, making him squeeze off another shot without aiming. The bullet entered the alien's skull through its slitted nose and out the back of its grey head, spraying purple gore. Its body dropped in a heap under the hatch.

Will walked over to the hatch, looking up at it from two-and-a-half feet away from his face. He knew he couldn't make that jump. He wasn't much of an athlete. He looked down at the body by his feet, getting an idea. He holstered his gun and stepped up on the giant's silver armored chest, being raised two feet off the gold walkway. He crouched down low, and jumped, catching the sides of the hatch but his fingers fell free from the smooth surface. He repeated the act until he was able to catch the sides and pull himself up. The smell of smoke and burning metal greeted his nostrils as he pulled himself up onto the surface of the sphere.

He pulled himself up through Maru's ship's hatch as the sphere beneath him shuddered from within. He quickly crouch ran toward the ship's cockpit, squeezing his way into the tiny seat that immediately adjusted to his much bigger size than its usual pilot.

"Biometric signature required," a computerized female voice said as a panel popped up beside what looked like the flight controls, a U-shaped steering wheel device. He put his hand on the panel, information flooding his brain as the ship's AI told him how to drive it. He worked his fingers across the ship's controls, disengaging the gravity tether Maru engaged to keep them linked together with the Plagueonian ship. He pulled on the flight wheel, pulling away from the grey spherical ship as it exploded from the inside, falling behind the rampaging monster in the city below.

13

New York City

Will watched from seven-hundred-feet up in the air as the monster known as Plague approached the wreckage of the crashed Plagueonian sphere that landed in the Civic Center. He inspected the wreckage, reeling back as a creature half his size sprang from it and unleashed a blast of some sort of green fire breath into his face. Plague stumbled back, destroying a big red building as the creature that attacked him landed on its five digit, razor sharp black claw tipped, armored feet.

Its saurian head looked up at its opponent, its green eyes blazing, its armor laden brows that stretched back to its horn-crested head furrowed, and sharp teeth bared. Its nostrils flared in anger, a horn protruding from its nose at the end of its squared snout. A small horn protruded from the monster's forehead, leading into the armored plates topping its head.

Jagged armored plates with green glowing spirals lined the smaller Kaiju's back, starting at the back of the monster's head and ending at the base of its tail. Three large bony jagged spikes protruded from each side in between the sides of the middle four plates.

A giant armored plate adorned the Kaiju's broad chest, glowing spirals reaching out from a green jewel on the middle of the plate. More armored plates reached down from the chest plate, ending at the bottom of the base of its tail, each decorated with two glowing green, squared spirals on each side.

Its shoulders were armored with plates running down to its elbow where a bundle of spikes protruded. Its forearms were armored as well, a chamber of some kind sitting atop its arm, ending at the Kaiju's wrists. They ended in armored, four digit hands, tipped with razor sharp, black claws.

Its legs were as heavily armored as the rest of the Kaiju's body, plates of armor running up its thighs from its knees which a giant spike protruded from. A tail whipped around behind the creature, wrapped in bony bands of armor, rippling with unnatural muscles and ending in a club-like structure with three spikes.

Will recognized the creature. The maroon color of his flesh and the dragon-like appearance was all he could recognize of what once was his three-foot-tall friend.

The monster standing before Plague was Marugrah.

Plague recovered, staring at the small but growing Kaiju standing before him. Will swore he could see Marugrah growing before his eyes. Plague roared, letting loose a torrent of fire from his maw, enveloping Marugrah. Once the flames faded, Marugrah stood smoldering but unharmed, thanks to his new heavily armored body. Marugrah let loose another blast of his green heat ray, striking Plague in the chest and throwing the larger creature back into a big white rectangular

building with the Verizon logo on it, demolishing some
weird X-shaped buildings as he fell through the Verizon
building.

While Plague struggled with his bulk, Marugrah
inspected his new body. He looked at his hands, his
body and his legs. Satisfied with what he saw, he let out
what Will could only guess as being a war cry before he
pounced on his larger foe, clawing at Plague's armored
chest. Plague grabbed Marugrah by the waist, searing
his armored flesh, as he rose to his feet and tossed the
smaller Kaiju across the city. Marugrah tumbled through
the decimated Civic Center, past Canal Street, and
coming to a stop in lower Manhattan.

Marugrah crawled out of the ruins of a few blocks of
city, about three-hundred-feet tall now. Whatever was in
that serum he was injected with was making him grow
rapidly. He roared defiantly at the flaming monster
charging through untold miles of concrete and steel
toward him. Marugrah charged himself, running at
Plague on his new thick, stocky legs. Marugrah turned
his body, lashing out at Plague with his long club-tipped
tail. The club hit Plague in his flaming face, throwing
the Kaiju to the ground of Little Italy with a yelp.

Maru grabbed at the armored plates on Plague's back,
pulling the larger creature to his knees. Plague tried to
reach back and grab Maru to no avail. He let go with one
hand of Plague's armored back, a bony spike erupting
from the chamber on his forearm. He plunged the spike
into Plague's unarmored side, eliciting a cry of pain
from the killing machine. Plague swung his arm around,
striking Marugrah in the side of the head. He stumbled
back, Plague's tail wrapping around his leg and pulling

him off his feet. Marugrah fell on his armored back, crushing buildings beneath his mass. Plague got to his feet, the hole in his side leaking black blood. Plague leaned down, grasping Marugrah's throat with his hands. Marugrah gurgled, unable to breath.

Not wanting to see his friend die, Will engaged the ship's weapon systems. He targeted Plague's back, pulling the trigger on the back of the flight wheel. Twin streams of yellow lasers erupted from the front of the oval craft, striking Plague's head. The Kaiju put his hands to his head, trying to block the annoying lasers. Will let go of the trigger as a warning icon blinked on the heads up display projected on the craft's windshield, indicating that the lasers were out of juice and needed to recharge. Plague removed his hands, looking to the sky for the source of the annoyance but found nothing as the ship was still cloaked.

The distraction was enough for the now four-hundred-foot Marugrah to catch his breath and push the Plagueonian-turned-Kaiju off of him and get to his feet. Plague got to his feet as well, shoulder charging Marugrah, the giant spikes that jut from his shoulder angled at Marugrah's chest. He side-stepped the charging monster, grabbing the biggest spike on Plague's shoulder as he passed. Plague didn't even try to stop, the spike being ripped from his shoulder in a spray of black, a tangle of sinews and veins dangling from the bottom of the spike. Plague fell to the ground, crying out in agony as he landed on his stomach atop the former New York Police Department HQ, a long building with a dome protruding from the middle along with a number of other buildings.

Plague tried to get to his feet, black blood gushing
from his shoulder but Marugrah was already atop him.
He grabbed at the plates lining Plague's back, peeling
them away as he squealed with anguish. Once he
removed most of the plates, he raised the spike he pulled
from Plague's arm and plunged it into the Kaiju's back.
Maru was probably estimating where the creature's heart
was, Will guessed. Plague squirmed and wailed until the
monster finally fell still.

Plague, the giant destroyer of worlds, was dead.

Just like that.

The battle went so fast, Will could hardly believe it
was really over after him having seemed invincible an
hour or so ago when he first arrived.

Marugrah threw his head to the sky and roared in
victory. Jets descended from the sky, firing at the last
monster standing.

"No!" Will yelled. "He's on our side!"

"Opening com channels," the AI said.

"Circling around for another pass. Aim for the
creature's legs," one of the pilots of the four F-22
Raptors that came out of nowhere.

"No! Disengage! He's on our side," Will said.

"What the fuck is a kid doing on the radio? This is a
military channel, get off the radio," the same pilot said.

"William? Is that you?" Angel's voice came over the
radio.

The pilots stayed silent, hearing Command's voice.

"Yeah, it's me," Will said. "Don't shoot. That is
Marugrah. I repeat, that creature is Marugrah."

"But how?" Angel asked.

"I'll explain once I return to HQ. Just don't fire at him,

please. He is in enough pain."

"Alright. All units, stand down."

"Roger that, Command," another pilot said. Will could tell he was holding back his anger at being told to abandon fighting something he obviously thought was a threat.

Will sat back in his seat, relieved as the F-22s broke away. Marugrah, seeing the jets leaving, followed the path of destruction from his fight with Plague back to the decimated Verizon building and the weird X-shaped buildings. He moved past them, heading for the waterway. He stepped into it, the water sloshing up to his knees. Seeing no other way around or just not caring, he plowed through the Brooklyn Bridge, one of the oldest suspension bridges in the United States. He made his way along the waterway to the Upper Bay, then the Lower Bay, before slipping into the ocean depths, where he would wait for the next Kaiju to show its ugly face.

Seeing Marugrah was gone, Will piloted the ship away from the decimated city of New York and back toward Washington, D.C. to his friends and allies. After a ten-minute ride at Mach 3, he located the CCU HQ and landed on its roof. No one could see the cloaked ship so Will didn't think it was a problem. He found the roof door, taking it down to the top floor that the command room was on. He walked in, everyone in the room turning toward him.

"Where the fuck have you been?" Ashley said, her face a mask of anger.

"Um, well...in a spaceship," Will said, being greeted with a slap to the face.

"I was worried about you. You just disappeared. You

didn't even tell us where you went. You could have been killed infiltrating that ship."

Will rubbed the side of his face, a red handprint forming. "Yeah, yeah. It was a bit of a dick move. I'm sorry. I'm fine. Plus, I got to see a Kaiju fight."

"Speaking of which, what happened to Marugrah? You said that giant red dragon was him," Cole said, stepping forward.

"Yeah...he turned himself into a Vexnoxtuque," Will said.

He did what? That fool! Marudon fumed, letting out an angry squawk. *There is no way he can fight the effects that the serum will have on his mind.*

"Are you saying the green stuff they pumped into him will drive him crazy?" Will asked.

Yes, that is what I am saying. Though, it is possible that he could fight it, now that I think of it. Plague seemed to have been able to. But that could have been because he was always a crazy lunatic, Marudon said.

"Maru looked like he lost it there for a moment when he was finishing off Plague," Will said, remembering the way Marugrah slowly killed Plague, as if he enjoyed the Kaiju's suffering.

"So, he may turn against us?" Cole asked.

"Let's hope he doesn't," Will said. "He's the only chance we have at getting through this thing alive."

THE INVASION

14

Washington, D.C.

After the battle in New York that left most of the city in
ruins, and some congratulations from Cole for a
successful mission, Will and his friends were escorted
back to the room they stayed in the night before by
Brice, an enthusiastic young soldier and a part of
Gamma squad.

"Here we are," Brice said, opening the door to the
room.

Everyone piled in, plopping down on the beds. It was
an exhausting and stressful day, especially for Will. He
aided his friend in becoming a Kaiju, an act that might
also make him go insane, and watched him battle and
kill another Kaiju. It wasn't something he wanted to do.
If he knew that was what Maru was going to do, he
would have stopped him before he flew off in his space
ship to New York.

Brice shut the door, leaving them alone in the room. It
was incredibly silent, everyone probably digesting the
day's events. A monster falling from the sky, destroying
the city, seemingly unstoppable, only to be killed hours
later. The worst part was, more Kaiju were on their way,
along with an alien army.

Will kicked off his shoes, trying to get comfortable on
the bed and thinking they might be in the room another
night.

"You think they'll let us go home soon to get some
fresh clothes? Or at least provide us with some? I could

really use a shower," Nicole said, breaking the silence as she looked down at herself with disgust.

"The world is at war with aliens. Whether we stink or not isn't their concern, I guess," Will said. "It'd be nice if they did, though. I smell as bad as that ferret I had years ago."

"I remember that. Johnny, right? I liked that little guy," Aaron chuckled.

A knock on the door made everyone groan.

"Better be a hot chick here to help alleviate my stress," Aaron yelled at the door.

The door opened and Jessica Evangeline, who insisted on being called by her callsign, Eva, walked in.

"I consider myself to be hot. And if you consider a nice shower and some fresh clothes a way to alleviate stress, then yes I am," she said. "You guys have earned it."

"I think I've earned a shower with you, baby," Aaron said, winking at Eva.

"If anyone has earned that, it is the man who infiltrated the enemy ship but he is kinda taken," Eva laughed.

Will felt his cheeks turning red, getting a glare from Aaron and a punch to his arm. He looked into the angry blue eyes of Ashley. He had only been with her two days, one of those days being attacked by a giant alien Kaiju, but he knew she had strong feelings for him as he does for her. It was weird how disaster scenarios brought people even closer together than they were before. Especially in a short amount of time of knowing each other.

"Don't worry about it, Ash. I'm just messing around,"

Eva said, calming the girl.

"I'm still available for yah," Aaron said, getting another laugh out of Eva.

She winked at him and motioned for them to follow her. They got up and followed her into the hallway. She pointed to doors saying each person's name as she came to them, their appointed rooms. She finally stopped at a door, only having Will and Ashley left, smiling wide.

"This room is for you two," she said, still smiling.

"Is there, like, two showers in the room?" Will asked, his cheeks starting to turn red again.

"Nope. Just one shower," she said, opening the door.

Will and Ashley walked into the room, Eva shutting the door behind them. The room was a third of the size of the room they spent last night in. It contained a single bed, a television set sitting atop a stand, a nightstand beside the bed, and a dresser. A door at the far side of the room was ajar, revealing a white bathroom with a sink, toilet and shower. It was simple but Will thought he could get used to it.

"So, you want to take one first?" Will asked, turning to the beautiful girl that he'd be sharing the room with standing next to him.

"Why don't you take one first," she said, looking at him with that heartwarming smile of hers.

"Alright," he said, kissing her softly on the lips.

He grabbed the clothes from the bed, and headed to the bathroom, shutting the door behind him. He shed his clothes and hopped into the tub. He closed the shower curtains and turned on the water, the warm liquid instantly relieving him as it hit his skin. He washed his body and hair after letting the water run over his body for a few minutes. He got out, toweled himself off and got dressed in tee-shirt and sweatpants. He thought about shaving but was too tired to even try. He emerged from the bathroom feeling a little better but not much.

"You always take a half hour shower?" Ashley asked with a grin, laying on the bed watching TV.

"Oh, give me a break. I fought aliens on their own space ship today. I even killed one," Will said, a sly smile of his own spread across his lips. "Your turn, princess. Trust me, it'll feel frigging magical."

"You're my hero, you know that. What you did was awesome. Sorry for slapping you. You scared me," she said, standing from the bed.

He embraced her, nuzzling her face.

"It's alright. I deserved it," he whispered into her ear.

He kissed her cheek and led her to the bathroom. She walked into the bathroom, shutting the door behind her. Will laid down on the bed as the water in the bathroom came on. He turned his attention from the images in his head, to the television. A show called *NCIS* was on. He used to watch the show a lot. He liked the characters, especially Abby, the hyper-forensic scientist. At some point during the show he must have dozed off, only to be awakened by someone sitting on his lower back, giving him the most amazing backrub he had ever had.

"Damn, you are so tense," Ashley said, revealing herself as the backrubber.

"Jeez, you are amazing at this," Will moaned.

He reached a hand back for the remote to shut off the television, his hand finding a smooth, unclothed leg instead.

"Are you...," he started but trailed off.

She lifted her body off of him, allowing himself to roll on his back. She sat back down on him, her naked form silhouetted by the glow of the TV, most of her was still cloaked in shadow but he could see her smile. Will could feel his face turning red. She put her hands on his shoulders, rubbing the tension out of them. He couldn't help but let out a moan of pleasure, getting a giggle out of her.

"What are you laughing at? This feels really damn good," he told her, trying not to look anywhere but her face.

"Yeah, I know. I took a class to be a masseuse, believe it or not," she said.

"That actually explains a lot."

Will felt the tension being rubbed from his body. Everything melted away. The threat of an incoming alien invasion. His friend possibly becoming an insane monster. The hundreds of soldiers that died today. All of it was gone. It was just him and Ashley.

She rubbed her bare legs against his sides, lifting his shirt up and making contact with his bare skin, sending a shiver through his body. She leaned down and kissed him, digging her nails into his chest and making it clear what she wanted. And after all that he had been through that day, he took comfort in her, easing away all his pent up stress.

He moved through the ocean, breathing easily in the salty water. But something was wrong. His mind was a mess. Struggling with an overwhelming madness threatening to overcome his mind. Threatening to turn him upon his friends. Upon humanity.

He fought it off, pushing it away in a mental battle for control as he stopped to rest on the ocean floor not far from Washington D.C. Fish swam by his giant face along with whales and sharks. His stomach growled. He reached out with one of his massive hands, catching a whale and depositing it in his maw where he devoured it. He cringed at the horrible taste, but it satiated his hunger.

With his hunger gone, he slept. But even as he did, he felt them. The Plagueonians. They were close. Moving past the planet called Mars. They would arrive at Earth by tomorrow and then the real battle would begin.

Just as Marugrah felt all this, so did Will.

Will awoke, feeling better than he had ever felt before. Mostly because of the amazing night he had with the beautiful girl lying beside him, tangled in the white bed sheets that hid her body, her smooth, peach colored legs sticking out from beneath them. He leaned down, nuzzling her sleeping face.

She groaned, obviously not wanting to start the day. Will didn't either but they had work to do. Like, getting ready for an alien invasion. Their harbinger may be dead, but the invaders are probably worse. He poked her face. She swatted his hand away, opening her eyes.

"Hey, handsome," she said with a smile.

"Hey, beautiful," he said with a smile of his own. "Time to get up."

"Let's just stay in bed. Let the world end," she groaned.

"I wish we could but I can't allow that to happen," he said.

The door to the room swung open, making Ashley squeal in surprise and cover herself up with the bed sheet.

"What the hell, dude? You got some last night, but not me? You friggin' suck," Aaron said, standing in the doorway.

"You ever heard of knocking, asshat?" Ashley growled.

"Of course I have, honey."

"Call me honey again, and I will rip your balls off, buddy."

"What do you want?" Will asked, breaking up the cat fight before it got worse.

"First, cover up your junk. I don't wanna see that shit. Second, I came to get you. Satellites picked up a large object moving past Mars," Aaron said, but his eyes said he was hiding something.

"Well, maybe it will teach you to knock. We'll be there soon," Will replied.

Aaron walked out of the room, shutting the door behind him, a haunted look on his face.

"Probably should've locked the door," Ashley said, shedding the bed sheet and slipping on some clothes.

"Yes, we should have," Will said, getting up from the bed and slipping on his own clothes, a black tactical uniform like Walker and Hlad wore the previous day. Ashley wore the same garb.

"You sure we're ready for something like this? I mean, two days ago I was regular girl, working at a coffee shop and you worked at a convenience store. We were just kinda thrown into this. It's a bit overwhelming," she said, looking at their new attire.

108

"Yeah, it is overwhelming. I can't quite wrap my head around this whole situation and what I've seen… And what is coming. But I have to put that stuff aside for now and help with what I can," Will said, finishing tying the laces on his boots.

The bed shifted as she crawled across it, putting her arms around him.

"You're so much more strong minded than I am," she said, kissing his neck.

He caressed the side of her face as she laid it on his shoulder.

"It takes years of practice. Especially when your parents were never around and you had to grow up faster than you should," he said. "Let's go."

"Alright," she said.

They walked out of their room, down the hall, and into the waiting elevator. Will pressed the button for the top floor. The doors shut and the elevator ascended a level, barely a thirty-second ride. They walked down the long hallway and entered the command room.

The first thing Will saw was the object, just passing the moon on the screen. The whale-like ship was easily recognizable to him as he had seen it in Maru's dream.

The Plagueonian mothership.

15

"I thought you said it was moving past Mars, not the fucking moon," Will said, his anger rising, still staring at the screen.

"Yeah, that was about...five hours ago. I didn't want you to rush up here. You went through enough yesterday," Aaron said, turning Will's attention toward him and his friends.

"I don't give a shit what I went through. I'm mentally tethered to a friggin' Kaiju. I'm never going to stop going through shit."

"Mentally tethered? You're connected to Marugrah?" Cole ask, sounding a little more excited than he should.

"Yeah. I know what he knows. Feel what he feels. It's really friggin' weird," Will said.

"Estimated time of arrival is three hours, sir," one of the console people said, interrupting their conversation.

"Not much time to prepare but at least we have something on our side that can help us stop it," Eva said.

Yes. A half mad Maruian will definitely be of help to us, Marudon said sarcastically, standing by Eva.

"He's not mad. He's fighting it and winning," Will said, the words slipping from his mouth without him even thinking.

Ashley squeezed Will's hand, snapping him out of a trance he seemingly slipped into. He was in Marugrah's mind for a moment as the creature woke up.

"Where is he?" Cole asked.

"The ocean still, but very close to here. Washington D.C.," Will said, squeezing Ashley's hand back.

"He's close and ready to help. That's good news."

"Question," Nicole said, interrupting the tactical input most probably about to come next, her long black hair pulled back in a tight pony tail. "Why are we dressed like your soldiers?"

"That is in case one or all of you knuckleheads want to

go flying around in a spaceship and infiltrate the enemy vessel again. Or if you want to help fight for your planet."

"Well, I know I'm not going to just sit in this damn place during the end of the world," Will said, meaning what he said. It could be his shared mind with Marugrah making him feel that way or it could be him really being tired of hiding from things he was afraid of. He had done that too much in his life. Either way, he wasn't going to sit by and do nothing while people fought for their lives and possibly died doing so.

"Screw that. I'm in no shape to fight a war nor do I want to," Walt said. Will knew the chubby man was right. He was disgusted with war and he could barely even run a half mile without passing out. He would have to sit this out.

"I'm in. Maybe I'll impress you, Eva," Aaron said, winking at the soldier woman. She just rolled her eyes, trying, and failing, to hide a smile. But Will knew the man was not just volunteering to possibly die to impress a girl. He was in for the same reason Will was: to protect the people he loved.

"I'm in if Will is in," Ashley said, wrapping her arms around Will's. He was about to argue with her about it, but he knew he couldn't ask her to stay here while he was out fighting for the planet. And if he died doing so while she was safe in here...well, he couldn't imagine how that'd make her feel.

"I don't think I could fight even if I tried. I'm out," Nicole said, stepping away. She was right. She was never a good fighter. Not that she ever had to fight. If she did, she'd call on Will or Aaron to scare them away.

"I'll...I'll stay with Nicole," Jamie said, grabbing Nicole's hand, getting a surprised look out of her. These last couple days must've brought them closer together as well.

Three of them in, three of them out.

"Alright, then. You three..." Cole pointed to Jamie, Nicole, and Walt, "...report back to your bunks. Feeds will be streamed to your televisions if you wish it. You three..." Cole pointed to Will, Aaron, and Ashley, "...report to Gamma in the armory. You will train with weapons and deploy with them. Chop, chop, people. We only have three hours to get this shit done."

Eva led Will, Aaron, and Ashley down the hall to the elevator. The four of them took the elevator down three floors to about the middle of the building. The doors opened, revealing the entire floor filled with metal racks full of weapons. Assault rifles. Shotguns. Rocket launchers. Sniper rifles. Will wasn't much of a gun guy, but he knew enough of the guns from playing Call of Duty. Brice, Hlad, Walker and Angel were in the middle of the room, sitting on a bench area between the two rows of racks of guns, cleaning and prepping weapons, dressed in black body armor.

"Morning, mates. Ready for war?" Walker asked, his Aussie accent thick. Will could only figure that it was thicker because of his nervousness.

"So you are the three that decided to help out? I would've only thought Will would have volunteered. I was mistaken. You three have guts," Angel said, setting a Steyr AUG assault rifle on the bench where she was sitting. She walked over to them, extending her hand to no one in particular. Will took her offer, shaking her hand. Aaron and Ashley did the same. Eva walked past them and disappeared into the lines of racks.

"Alright. Let's get you armored up and then we'll see about weapons," Angel said turning to the nearest rack, pulling off a tactical vest with a white CCU stenciled on it like the one he wore when he infiltrated the Plagueonian sphere. She handed it to Will. He slid it on, tightening the vest's straps. She handed one to Aaron and Ashley. They put the vests on as they followed Angel walking past racks, looking at their contents. She pulled off a futuristic looking gun and handed it to Ashley who gave her a questioning look.

"That, my dear, is a KRISS Vector submachine gun. It fires .45 caliber APC rounds with little to no recoil. Wherever you aim, the bullets will hit," Angel explained before rooting through the weapon racks again.

She picked out another weapon and handed it to Aaron. "A FN SCAR-H battle rifle. It fires powerful 7.62x51 millimeter NATO bullets from a twenty round magazine."

She looked through the racks one last time, plucking another weapon and handing it to Will. "A M4 carbine. A shorter and lighter version of the M16A2 assault rifle. It fires 5.56x45 millimeter NATO rounds. It is capable of firing in semi-automatic or in three-round bursts. Whatever suits your fancy."

"Now that everyone has a weapon, let's try them out," she said, leading them to the shooting range also installed on the floor. Now that Will looked around, the whole floor looked to be soundproofed.

"Sounds fun! Eva, wanna help me out?" Aaron asked, raising his eyebrows three times at her.

Walker, Hlad, and Brice busted out laughing as Eva leveled a sinister glare at him, making Aaron turn away from her.

"There is no way you're gonna 'hit that' as the kids say these days," Angel said, putting a hand on his shoulder. "The boys have tried and gotten broken bones for it."

Will and Ashley looked at each other, busting up laughing themselves.

"I hate you guys," Aaron growled, looking discouraged but Will knew he wouldn't give up that easily.

"Oh, whatever, man," Will laughed.

Will walked up to the long table in front of the range which was an enclosed section of the floor at the far end. Targets of a silhouetted person hung from the ceiling. He picked up a pair of earphones that would block the loud report of the gunfire. He took aim at the target's head, aiming through the weapon's ACOG scope. He pulled the trigger, the M4 bucking in his hands. To his surprise, he hit his target.

"Damn, dude," Aaron said, stunned at Will's accuracy.

"Where the bloody hell did you learn to shoot?" Walker asked, just as stunned.

"I used to hunt with my dad. Deer and stuff," Will replied, adjusting the earphones. He took aim again, firing off two more shots, each hitting their mark. He switched to three-round burst mode, firing at the same spot with the same accuracy.

"My turn," Aaron said, putting on some earphones. Will stepped back with Angel and Ashley as Aaron took aim. Will watched him fire off seven shots, each of them missing the target. Will couldn't help but chuckle. The women beside him giggled, too. Aaron growled, emptying the SCAR's twenty-round clip, only hitting the target four times. In the chest.

"I suppose that's a good start. Try aiming more. Measure your shots," Eva said, walking over to Aaron. She pulled out her handgun, a SIG Sauer P226, firing three shots, each hitting the target's head.

"That...was so hot," Aaron said, looking dreamily at Eva. She patted him on the face and walked back to the bench area, Walker and Brice making whooping sounds at Aaron.

Ashley walked up to the firing range, not even attempting to put on the earphones. She took aim and pulled the trigger on her KRISS. The target's head was torn apart, falling from the clamp that held it aloft. The thirty-round clip was emptied in a matter of seconds. She turned back to the group, a smile on her face.

"That was so awesome!" she exclaimed.

"Well it seems you two are just fine with your weapons. Sir Flirtsalot needs some work. Feel free to practice some more if you like. Make sure you stock up on ammo and be ready when the order to move out is given," Angel said, turning back to her team. She sat down on the bench, continuing to look over her AUG.

Aaron reloaded his SCAR, took aim, and fired off a shot, hitting the target's chest. Will turned away from his friend practicing to kill eight-foot-tall aliens and toward the racks of weapons. He located the area Angel took the M4 from and procured a few magazines, stuffing them in the vest's pockets. Ashley did the same for her KRISS. Armed to the teeth, even with a knife sheathed on their chests, Will and Ashley sat on the bench.

"You know you didn't have to volunteer to come with me. Maru pulled me into this and I pulled you in," Will said, staring at the floor.

"Yeah, well, I felt I did. It's like you said, it's better to fight than to hide," she said, putting her hand in his.

"Yeah, it is."

The three-hour wait seemed like an eternity. Aaron spent the time practicing with his SCAR while everyone else watched the news, waiting for someone to spot the giant ship approaching the Earth. Then it came. The image of the giant grey whale-looking ship descending from the sky over San Francisco. A hatch on its underside opened, discharging a chrysalis like the one that landed in New York City that carried Plague. The chrysalis split open, revealing a three-tailed, lion-like beast that looked as if it were wearing bones as armor. Will had seen that beast as well in Maru's dream.

"Cerberus," Will said.

"It doesn't have three heads," Brice pointed out.

"Yeah, but it does have three tails," Ashley said, understanding Will's reasoning for the name. The creature also looked like it could be the guard dog of Hell. "How about Cerboura. It's a mix of Cerberus and *oura* which is Greek for 'tail'."

Angel relayed the name to Cole.

"Command to all fire teams. Contact in San Francisco. Target's code-name is 'Cerboura'. Everyone report to designated transportations. Command out," Cole's voice came over Will's earpiece, and undoubtably everyone else's.

"Alright, Gamma, let's move out!" Angel said, standing and slinging her AUG over her back via the gun's strap.

Will peeled his eyes away from the television showing panicking people running for their lives in the San Francisco streets, stood and followed the five soldiers walking toward the elevator, Ashley and Aaron close behind him. The team split up to use the elevator. The first ride was Brice, Hlad, Walker and Eva. Ten minutes later, Angel, Will, Ashley, and Aaron got on the elevator. They rode it down, the doors opening to the hotel-like lobby where Eva and the other guys of Gamma team waited. They walked across the white linoleum floor and out the door to two waiting tan military Humvees.

Will climbed into the back seat of the second Humvee, Ashley sliding in beside him. Angel hopped in behind the wheel, starting the vehicle as Aaron jumped in the passenger seat. Angel pulled away from the faux hotel, following the Humvee in front of them, driven by Hlad. She followed him from Buzzard Point to Fort Lesley J. McNair a few blocks from the CCU HQ that housed a big swath of green land with a waiting black Boeing CH-47 Chinook transport helicopter.

The other fire teams were already aboard, waiting for the last team. The Chinook had a maximum capacity of fifty troops but the CCU's forces only contained thirty-eight. Not nearly enough to combat the forces invading San Francisco but they will have help from the National Guard and other military troops already in the city, mostly providing expertise and support.

They exited the vehicles, running to the helicopter.

They hopped in a single file line through the loading ramp at the chopper's caboose, Will bringing up the rear. The inside of the chopper was spacious but at the same time crowded. Armored men and women sat on the seats lining the chopper's inside, their gazes intimidating. Will sat down next to Ashley and buckled in as the chopper lifted off the ground and the loading ramp lifted up, closing with a clunk.

Will's stomach swirled, nervous about the coming battle and whether he could help stop the end of the world or not.

San Francisco

"Son of a bitch," Samantha Snader muttered as someone bumped into her, making her spill her cooled coffee on the new dress she wore. "Watch where you're going, fuck head."

"Sorry lady," the man who bumped into her said nervously.

"You're lucky I don't charge you for my dry cleaning, buddy," she growled, fixing the man with a sinister glare. The man walked away at a fast pace, trying to avoid a confrontation.

Samantha sighed and continued on her way home from her daily college classes when the boom of something rapidly entering the atmosphere sounded from the San Francisco sky. She looked up to see a gigantic gray ship that almost looked like a giant sky whale descending from the sky. The ship ejected some sort of object which landed a few blocks away from where she stood on the cross section of Market Street and South Van Ness street. She couldn't see the object from street level but she heard screams and the sound of crumbling buildings along with a roar unlike anything she had ever heard. It was almost like a Dubstep mixed lion roar.

She saw the footage from New York City of the monster, or 'Kaiju' as the officials called it, that landed in Central Park. That thing was horrifying and as she saw the creature that landed in San Francisco, which was maybe a hundred feet shorter than the New York monster and twice as long, charge through the street the next block over, she screamed, everyone in the street beside her joining in. It was even scarier than the New York monster, Plague, as well. The Kaiju stopped, turning toward the screaming, and now fleeing people in the street, decimating the castle-like San Francisco City Hall building with its three tails along with the round corner of the Lois M. Davies Symphony Hall building and a few smaller buildings under its front legs at the four-way intersection it stood upon.

Samantha remained locked where she was standing in fear. The Kaiju seemed to consider the fleeing people around her with curiosity. And then disdain. She saw it in the monster's burning red reptilian eyes. It took a step forward, crushing cars beneath its massive bone white armored paws. Its jaw dropped open, revealing rows of needle-like teeth, letting out another loud bellow, making her cover her ears.

The creature pushed further down Van Ness Street still

two blocks away, its wide shoulders with giant spikes jutting out of them plowing through the buildings on either side of the street, raining debris upon the streets and anyone unlucky enough to be under it. A missile came out of nowhere, striking the monster in the back. Samantha looked to the sky as an F-22 Raptor roared overhead. Then another. And another. Each raining down missiles upon the behemoth. The last missile to strike the monster along with its angry growl triggered her flight instinct, running the best she could while wearing stiletto heels with the flow of humanity away from the giant armored quadrupedal Kaiju.

People shoved and bounced her around as she ran, making her stumble, but she never stopped. She didn't want to die. The angry wails of the Kaiju, the boom of exploding missiles, and the sound of crumbling buildings echoed behind her as a war was waged. Then the flowing river of people abruptly stopped, Samantha bumping into the backs of two people in front of her.

"What is it?" she asked, her voice cracking with fright.

Only screams answered her as more people were killed from an unknown source. Mangled bodies flew through the air, one landing next to her with a wet splat that made Samantha sick to her stomach. Seeing the torn open body with a baseball sized hole in its chest along with the smell of burning flesh made her discharge her stomach contents. When she looked up, the remaining people in the street were dispersing, running left and right down Otis Street. She ran left, following the smaller crowd and catching a glimpse of the killers. Eight-foot-tall creatures in silver armor covered in symbols she had never seen before fired yellow lasers from a futuristic looking rifle at the fleeing people.

A woman in front of her dropped to the street, a hole through her chest. Samantha hopped over the woman, one of the heels on the stilettos snapping and making her fall on her face. She didn't bother getting back up.

Maybe if I stay still and play dead, they won't bother with me, she thought.

She hoped her idea would work. She didn't want to die. She was a year away from finishing college, had an okay job, and was seeing a really sweet guy. She didn't want to leave any of that.

If I survive this, it might all be gone anyway, she thought, tears streaming down her cheeks.

Metal on concrete clanged loudly next to her head but out of her sight. She couldn't see what was there but had no doubts it was one of the silver armored beings. She heard it say something in a language she had never heard before. Nobody probably had heard it before. The things prowling the streets were alien. She had no doubt about that.

Something blazing hot touched her back. It took everything she had not to scream out in pain. Somehow, she remained still, faking death. She heard the creature grunt in what might have been satisfaction and walk away, its metal feet clanging on the asphalt road. She let out the breath she had been holding, sucking in fresh air but never daring to get up. She listened to the sounds of explosions, crumbling buildings, and the wails of the Kaiju. It sounded like the military was bombarding the creature with everything they had in an effort to kill it. But they had no luck against the one in New York. It took another creature that suddenly appeared to take down the monster that was known as Plague.

After a few moments of not hearing the eight-foot aliens, she stood from her spot and ran the opposite way she heard the aliens go. It was hard for her to run with a broken heel. One of the aliens must have seen her, because laser blasts rippled around her feet as she ran. One struck her leg, felling her to the hard asphalt, ripping apart the skin on her hands and knees but the pain from that was nothing compared to the searing hole in her leg.

Tears flooded from her eyes harder as she backed away from the approaching alien that shot her on her hands and good leg. It was all for naught. The alien leveled its gun at her head. She begged the creature to be spared but it didn't listen or didn't care as it fired the gun, creating a hole through her head, destroying her brain, killing her instantly.

17

They were kept up to date on the events in San Francisco. The military were holding their own against Cerboura. Plagueonian troops were dropped into the city and were exterminating the city's population. The military dropped their own troops to combat the aliens. That was where the fire teams of the CCU would help out first. Will could feel Marugrah making his way to San Francisco via the ocean and any other waterway he could fit his bulk through.

He felt the Chinook transport helicopter descend,

dropping toward their landing zone. The loading bay door at the helicopter's rear opened, the space flooding with the sound of battle and the smell of smoke, making everyone cough as they stood and exited the chopper in two lines onto a baseball field a couple miles from Cerboura. The mothership was gone, but several smaller crafts that looked like miniature versions of the mothership zipped through the sky, targeting the jets and helicopters in the sky. It was a miracle one of them didn't fire upon the transport chopper they were on.

Will formed up with Gamma squad, checking their comms before looking over their weapons.

"Everyone ready?" Angel asked.

"Everything is in order Captain," Hlad said.

"Alright, let's mov…" Angel was cut off as a yellow beam shot from the sky above them, puncturing the helicopter's fuel tank, sending it up in a ball of fire that threw the soldiers several feet from it to the ground. The soldiers closest to the blast were consumed by the fire or had pieces from the obliterated chopper embedded in their bodies.

Will picked himself off the grassy ground, his skin singed, his body aching. He looked to see Ashley in the same condition as well as Aaron.

"Holy *shitballs*," Walker said, looking at the wreckage.

"We have to move. That ship will be back," Eva said, hefting up a Barrett M82 sniper rifle as she got up from the ground.

"Eva's right. All callsigns fall out," Angel said, making her way out of the flaming ballfield and onto Turk Street.

Will led Ashley and Aaron after the charging soldiers of Gamma squad who ran the opposite way of the battle between Cerboura and the United States military.

"Where are we going?" Will yelled.

"We're meeting up with the soldiers helping to evacuate the city," Brice said, unslinging his SPAS-12 tactical shotgun from his back.

They ran, entering the Fillmore district, a horde of armed Plagueonians occupying the area. They skidded to a halt, bringing up their weapons and opening fire on the aliens. Will was able to take down three creatures, aiming for their exposed faces under the helmet atop their head like he did in the ship he infiltrated with Maru. Seeing the effectiveness, everyone else followed his lead, allowing them to quickly mow down the invaders.

"Hell yes!" Aaron whooped as he reloaded his SCAR.

They pushed through to Steiner Street, turning south, the sound of an exploding jet sounding throughout the city. They followed the street down to Alamo Square Park, which was crawling with soldiers and civilians. A Chinook descended on the far side of the park, its loading ramp lowering. People swarmed into the helicopter's ass end, clawing and shoving their way to get aboard. Will found it horrifying how people acted in a time of chaos. People were trampling over others, killing more than the Plagueonians and Cerboura were.

Angel caught a soldier by the shoulder who looked at her, horror etched into his young face. He was no older than Will was.

"Who's in charge?" she asked him.

"Colonel Jacobs," the soldier said, his voice shaky.

"Where is he?"

He pointed to an older man in full combat gear standing on the side of the park apart from everyone else. They followed Angel as she walked over to the colonel.

"Colonel Jacobs," Angel said, getting the colonel's attention.

"Ah, the specialists. I thought you guys were dead after seeing that explosion at your LZ. It's a fucking disaster here. People are killing themselves to get out of the city and soldiers are being killed fighting the monster destroying the city, not to mention the fucking aliens killing every human they see," Jacobs ranted, catching his breath when he was finished.

"We know all about it, Colonel."

"Right. You guys are the experts. You killed the monster in New York, right?"

"Well, that was the work of another Kaiju that killed Plague," Will chimed in.

"What? Some kind of good monster that's on our side?" Jacobs asked.

"I suppose you could say that."

"Then where the fuck is it? Why isn't it here fighting the one here?"

"He's on his way."

Jacobs shook his head like he didn't believe Will and turned back to Angel. "We need to get these people out of here without them killing each other."

"That's gonna be hard to do. These people are scared shitless," Walker said, watching the Chinook take off.

"Yeah, well I'm scared shitless. So are my men. In case you didn't know, giant monsters and invading aliens are scary as fuck."

"I second that statement," Aaron said, agreeing with the colonel.

Will thought everything going on today and what happened yesterday was 'scary as fuck' too, but didn't voice it. He knew Ashley was probably feeling the same way. He wanted to grab her hand or to comfort her in some way but they were in the middle of a war and he didn't see a trace of fear on her face. She was stronger than she looked for sure.

"Contacts!" someone said, snapping Will's mind back to the battle. "East side!"

Will turned, gun at the ready, seeing a horde of Plagueonians flooding into the park the way he and the rest of Gamma squad entered. Bullets and laser bolts flew through the air as the two species engaged one another. Will took aim, firing his M4 in one shot mode to conserve ammo. He was able to drop a few Plagueonians before one of the alien assholes got lucky and hit a few of Jacob's men. After that, the shootout became a massacre. More soldiers dropped around Will, luckily none of them part of his team, not that he was enthusiastic about the men dying.

Will pulled Ashley behind the trees in the middle of the park, taking cover. Aaron, Angel, Walker, Hlad, and Brice did the same. Some of the soldiers did the same as well, forming a protective blockade in front of the civilians that were still present in a large circular patch of grass surrounded with rocks and waiting for another transport out of the city. Will leaned around the tree, firing off a few shots and killing two of the giant aliens, but dozens still remained.

"We've got reports on a second Kaiju making its way through Baja, California," a voice said through Will's earpiece. His mind inadvertently slipped from San Francisco to Baja. Marugrah rose from the Delfin Basin and made his way across desert and mountains, heading for the ocean on the other side faster than seemed possible for a creature his size and mass.

"Monitor, but do not engage. I repeat, do not engage. He's friendly," Cole's voice came through Will's ear piece as his mind slipped back into his own body.

"Will!" Ashley yelled, pulling him down as a laser bolt flew through the space he was just a split second before. "Keep your head in the game or you'll lose it."

"Sorry. Wasn't in my right mind for a moment," Will said, getting to his feet.

He took aim, emptying his clip into the advancing horde of armored invaders, killing four of them and injuring a dozen more. He was only doing part of the work. More were being dropped by everyone else firing their weapons, not to mention Eva's expert sniping. With each shot she fired, one of the Plagueonians' heads disappeared in a cloud of purple gore. Walker's FN Minimi light machine gun was also doing a good job mowing down the horde. The standard weaponry was just doing a fraction of the damage they were causing.

Will reloaded his M4, glancing over to see Ashley reloading her KRISS which had a higher rate of fire and was probably getting low on ammo by now. If that happened, she'd only have her hand gun and he didn't think that would be very effective at this range. He peeked out from behind the tree again, firing his rifle, only about ten Plagueonians left. Maybe seeing so many of their own killed by humans and knowing that the fight was a lost one or just wanting to preserve their lives, they turned tail and ran, exiting the park and running back the way they came.

"That's right alien assbags. Run!" Aaron yelled after them.

"Don't get too cocky, Charming," Eva said, watching the giants run up the street.

"Charming?" Aaron asked, confused.

"Yeah. After Prince Charming, the flirty guy from *Shrek*," Eva said with a big grin. "It's your callsign. I thought hard on it."

"I hate you," he grumbled.

"Sure. That's why you keep flirting with me," she said with a wink.

The chop of a helicopter cut off their banter and made Will look to the sky. Another Chinook fell from the sky, landing behind where he, Gamma squad, the soldiers, and civilians were standing. The soldiers escorted the remaining civilians to the helicopter, trying to prevent them from trampling over one another. They half succeeded as no one was killed. People may have some broken bones, though.

Will watched the chopper ascend into the sky. It was almost away when a yellow laser bolt shot from a ship no one heard arrive. The chopper exploded in a ball of fire, landing on the apartment buildings on the south side of the park, decimating their first floors, the people aboard the chopper dead. Men, woman, children, all meeting a fiery end.

"Those fucking monsters!" Jacobs yelled before being vaporized by another laser.

"Sir!" the young soldier they met when they first entered the park yelled, running toward where Jacobs stood, getting vaporized himself.

"Holy shit," Ashley gasped in horror.

"We need to get out of here," Brice said, reloading his shotgun.

"Right. On my mark, we run for those buildings," Angel said, motioning to the round fronts of the apartment buildings to their left, on the south side of the park. "1..."

"2..."

He glanced at Ashley who gave him a nod, indicating she was ready.

"3..."

He glanced at Aaron who flashed him a thumbs up, also ready to go.

"Go, go, go!"

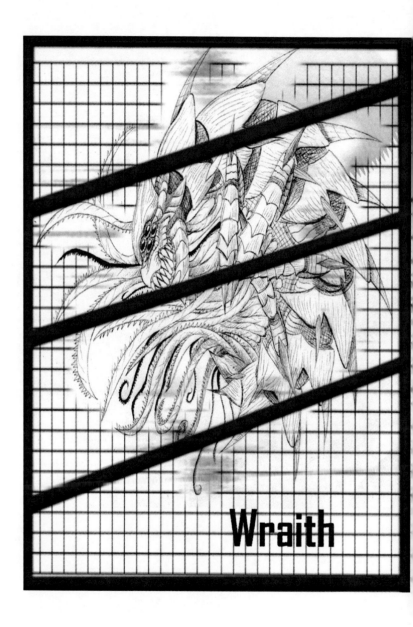

Wraith

18

Washington, D.C.

"We've got reports of a third Kaiju in Tokyo," Hannah Boyd said, bringing up footage of a giant gleaming white spider-like creature with long squid-like tentacles lining the monster's underside rising from Tokyo Bay from the console she sat at in the control room. Cole estimated the monster to be 400-feet-long and 200-feet-tall.

"Dear god," Cole said, horrified at the new monster. He thought Plague and Cerboura were horrifying, but with each new Kaiju the Plagueonians deployed, they got even more horrifying. "Is the ship there too?"

"No, it just left, sir. Disappeared into thin air, the reports say, just like in San Francisco."

"Shit. We need a way to track that ship."

"It's an alien ship. I don't know how we could track something like that. I'm no scientist, though."

Cole pondered the idea. If they could find a scientist to help them figure out how to track the ship, they could evacuate cities before it arrives and dropped a Kaiju on them. But how many did they have at their disposal? Could they find someone to figure it out in time? He doubted it. In a few hours, the ship had traveled from San Francisco to Tokyo. No one knew where it was going to strike next.

Then he remembered Marudon was in the room with him.

"Marudon, you think you could track the ship?" Cole

asked.

Maybe. If their ships work anything like I think they do, Marudon said. *But, I don't have the technology with me to do so.*

"Not even in your ship?"

We'd have to scrap the entire ship for me to build something like that and that would take time. They might appear again and drop another Kaiju. Or two more. Who knows.

"Yes, but the ship seems to cloak itself. The device you would build would help us locate it so we can take it down."

Marudon seemed to ponder the idea and then nodded, agreeing to the idea. She hopped out of the room accompanied by one of the technicians, heading to the building's roof where the ship resided.

Cole turned back to the screen, the Kaiju crawling out of Tokyo Bay and into the city. The way energy seemed to radiate from the creature's body made the thing look ghost-like.

"The Kaiju in Tokyo is to be known as 'Wraith' from now on," he said, giving the monster a name. Names helped when keeping track of more than one monster, he found. 'Wraith' was a Scottish dialectal word for 'ghost' and 'spirit', the name fitting the Kaiju's ghostly appearance.

"Roger. The Japanese Self Defense Force is mobilizing as we speak," Boyd said, her hands pushing her head phones tighter against her ears as she listened to the chatter.

"I'm not sure how much luck they will have but *maybe* they can stop it. It looks like most of its armor is on its legs, back, and face. If they hit it on its underside, maybe they can wound it."

"Relaying that information to them."

While Boyd, fluent in several languages, relayed the information to the JSDF in Japanese, Cole watched as Wraith plowed through Tokyo International Airport, crushing buildings and planes with a roar. Thin tentacles erupted from its mouth, probably what served as the creature's tongue, snatching up people fleeing from the monster, pulling them into its mouth. Once they retracted into the mouth, the creature began to chew. The sight sent his stomach swirling with disgust, making him want to upchuck. He could only imagine the sounds of crunching bones and shredding flesh coming from the monster's maw.

The people in the airport occupied Wraith, allowing four Bell AH-1 Huey Cobra attack helicopters to sneak up on the Kaiju from the south, deployed from Yakosuka Naval Base. The Kaiju didn't even notice their approach, snatching up the last remaining people alive in the decimated airport. They unleashed a torrent of Hydra 70 rockets and TOW missiles upon Wraith's back. It looked up from the ruins of the airports, turning its attention toward its attackers. The Cobras spread out, firing 20mm rounds from a M197 3-barreled gatling gun mounted under the craft's nose. Wraith twisted and bucked under the assault but it seemed more agitated than hurt. It opened its mouth wide, the mass of black tendrils reaching out and wrapping around one of the Cobras. The tendrils pulled the chopper into the monster's maw where it was crushed and shredded, erupting in a ball of flames in the Kaiju's mouth.

Wraith spat the crushed and flaming chopper out, where it landed in a crumpled heap in the airport ruins. The Cobras ducked and weaved, trying their best to avoid the mass of tendrils Wraith kept launching at them. Mitsubishi F-2A fighter jets roared into view, firing 20mm rounds from their JM61A1 rotary cannons into the mass of black tendrils, severing a few. The mass retracted into Wraith's sharp-toothed maw, letting out a cry of pain.

They actually managed to hurt a Kaiju! Cole cheered in his head.

Wraith watched the jets pass overhead, turning around for another pass, probably with missiles this time. It kept its eight eyes locked on the approaching jets. The jets launched AIM-9 Sidewinder air-to-air missiles, AIM-7 Sparrows air-to-air missiles, and Mitsubishi AAM Type 90 air-to-air missiles at the monster. The missiles hit the creature, obscuring it from view in smoke and flame. The pilots weren't even able to see the black mass of tendrils reach out of the smoke until it was too late. Two of the jets were enveloped and pulled from the sky. The cloud of smoke cleared, allowing Cole to see them crushed in its massive jaws.

The two remaining Cobras restarted their attack, launching more rockets, missiles, and 20mm rounds at the massive Kaiju's lower body, trying to hit its underside. Unfortunately, they were unable to hit the presumably soft flesh, their rounds just embedding themselves in or ricocheting off the hard armor on Wraith's legs and face. Thick tendrils erupted from underneath the overlapping plates on its back, lashing out at the choppers, felling one. The crushed chopper fell into the ocean, sinking to the bottom with the pilot, unknown if he was alive or dead. If he was still alive, it'd be a horrible way to die.

Cole turned away from the massacre projected on the screen.

"They don't stand a chance," Boyd gasped.

"ETA on the bomber heading to San Francisco?" Cole asked.

"It has just about reached its target. Nobody is within the blast zone."

The footage on the screen changed from Wraith oblitterating the JSDF to Cerboura decimating San Francisco. The creature stopped, looking to the sky as an object fell toward the Kaiju. The screen was blotted out by a bright white light that made everyone in the room turn away from it. When the white cleared, a giant mushroom cloud rose from the area Cerboura stood a moment before.

The cloud soon evaporated, revealing a mile-wide crater of burnt and melted city. The center shifted, bulged upwards, and burst apart, revealing a relatively unharmed Cerboura. It roared angrily at the sky as the bomber peeled away.

"Well, now we know for sure the MOAB doesn't work. If that doesn't work, I don't know what will," Cole said, looking at the screen in horror as Cerboura made its way out of the blackened ring.

19

San Francisco

Will ran, following the rest of the group consisting of the Gamma soldiers, the three remaining men from Jacob's team, and his two friends as they headed for the apartment buildings, slipping in between them. He felt heat tickle the back of his neck as a laser bolt hit the building at his back, throwing chunks of debris at his back. He was out of breath by the time they reached the back of the building.

"Holy...fucking...shit," Aaron wheezed between breaths as they huddled between a white and gray apartment building and a big white warehouse-looking building.

"That was close," Hlad said, looking around the corner, seemingly unaffected by the sprint from the park to where they now stood.

He is either superhuman or in really good shape, Will thought with a chuckle.

An angry wail from Cerboura echoed through the city again, the ground rumbling under their feet. The Kaiju was on the move. The military failed at containing the monster.

"We've got reports of a third Kaiju in Tokyo," a woman's voice said, her name was Hannah Boyd if Will remembered right, keeping them up to date on the emergence of yet another giant creature.

"Awh, give me a bloody break," Walker groaned.

"There is nothing we can do for Tokyo, but maybe we

can help out here with Cerboura," Angel said, looking around Hlad and back the way they came.

"They following us?" Will asked.

"No, but that ship is still there, waiting for us to pop back out," Angel said.

"That's just freaking great," Brice muttered.

"What do we do?" Ashley asked.

"Run for it again?" Hlad suggested.

"Well, sitting around here talking isn't going to get us anywhere," one of the soldiers said, her name tag reading M. Grimm.

"Obviously, but where the hell are we going to go? We're pinned down," Brice growled at Grimm, starting to freak out. Will knew if their minds unraveled, things would go to hell really quick. People would die.

Eva knew that, putting a calming hand on Brice's shoulder, making the man calm down some.

"I have an idea," another soldier whose tag read J. Snyder said.

"And what's that?" Angel asked, open to anything at that point.

"I have a smoke grenade. Maybe we could use that to help us escape to the next block over," Snyder said, holding out the device.

"Well, it's better than nothing," Angel said, taking the grenade from him.

They made their way around the warehouse, staying close to its sides and looked across the parking lot in front of it.

"Everyone ready?" Angel asked, glancing back at the gaggle of people behind her.

Everyone replied in the affirmative.

"Good. Didn't have a choice if you weren't anyways," she said, pulling the pin and chucking the grenade across the parking lot, landing at its edge. It detonated, releasing a cloud of white smoke.

"Go, go, go!" Angel yelled, running across the parking lot and into the expanding cloud of smoke.

Will ran after her, everyone else following Angel's lead. He ran through the smoke, coughing as he did, laser bolts flying through the air around them. He stumbled into a garden, a tree obscuring them from the ship's view. He moved deeper within the thick garden that almost seemed like a small jungle, regrouping with Angel. The rest of the group joined them, minus two.

"We good?" Angel asked.

"Grimm and Snyder are gone, Captain," the last remaining soldier of Jacob's squad said, her name tag reading M. Jones.

"Son-of-a-bitch," Angel muttered, shaking her head. "I don't mean to sound harsh, but we don't have time to mourn their deaths or anyone's for that matter."

"I understand. It's war, ma'am," Jones replied, tears in her eyes.

Will felt bad for the woman. She knew the people who died back in Alamo Park. They had been slaughtered like animals, but seemed to be taking it pretty well. Laser bolts started falling from the sky around them, making them duck for cover. Will looked around, seeing a window. He kicked at it, the glass breaking beneath his boot. He jumped through, the rest of the group jumping after him. They landed in someone's bed room, feeling like they were intruding but it was empty of any life and they weren't getting peppered with laser bolts from an alien spaceship anymore.

A boom echoed through the city, following by a wave of heat. The ship stopped its assault, no doubt seeing something they could not.

"What in the hell was that?" Eva asked.

"Sounded like a bomb..." Angel said, her eyes squinted in suspicion.

"Did...did they just drop a MOAB on our heads?" Ashley asked.

"I don't think Cole is that much of an asshole to do that to everyone in the city," Hlad said, sounding confident in the CCU Director. Will had no doubts that the man would do such a thing, though.

"Forget that. What are we going to do now? We're stuck, thanks to that bloody ship. Anyone got an RPG or a grenade launcher?" Walker asked.

"I have a grenade launcher," Jones said, holding up her M16 assault rifle, a grenade launcher attachment mounted under the gun's barrel.

"Maybe we can take that ship down with it," Walker said, reaching his hands out for the gun.

Jones handed the gun to him. "How?"

"Aim for its engines or thrusters."

"Does it even have those?"

"I guess we'll find out," Hlad said. "I'll distract the ship while you fire the grenade."

"Are you kidding me? You'll be killed!" Will said, a shocked expression on his face. The man looked too big to be very agile. He'd be killed in an instant.

"Don't underestimate the 'Wolf'," Angel said.

Will was confused by the name at first, but realized that was Hlad's callsign.

Walker and Hlad jumped out the window, disappearing into the jungle-like garden.

"The 'Dingo' and the 'Wolf'," Eva laughed.

Will glanced at Ashley, her face stoic. She saw him looking at her, and gave him a faint smile. He smiled back, feeling calmer about their situation. He wasn't calm about being incinerated by laser blasts from an alien ship, but more with being stuck in an apartment building with an alien ship lurking outside and not dead.

An angry roar shook the building.

There's also that, Will thought, tensing up again.

The sound of laser blasts striking asphalt echoed from the broken window, followed by the *poonk* of a fired grenade. An explosion filled the air, followed by the floor beneath their feet shaking violently. Will realized Hlad and Walker- or should he refer to them as Wolf and Dingo on mission?- did it. They took down the Plagueonian ship.

What badasses, Will thought, awed as the two men appeared at the window.

"All clear, Cap," Wolf said.

"Good job boys," Angel said, turning to the group behind her. "Let's go."

Will followed Angel out the window, Ashley right behind him. Then Aaron. Then Eva. Then Brice. Jones was the last to exit the building. Dingo handed Jones back her M16 which she shouldered with a nod. They walked out of the garden and into the street, seeing the destroyed ship. It destroyed the tall tower connected to the circular building attached to another building next to the warehouse they hid behind just ten minutes ago when it crashed. The back end was blown to crap, yellow fire billowing out of the destroyed grey hull.

"Shit yeah, guys!" Aaron whooped.

A crash spun them around. Cerboura stood in the next block over, destroying buildings. No military aircraft were in sight. They were either all destroyed or ran out of ammo or fuel. The land beyond the block the Kaiju stood in was a blackened crater.

That asshole Cole did *drop a MOAB on their head,* Will fumed.

Cerboura lifted his skulled head, his jaws looking as if they were chewing on something. Will thought the creature could be male with its broad chest.

Is he...eating people? Will wondered, the image making his stomach swirl with disgust. Then the sound of shredding flesh and grinding bones filled his ears, making him throw up what food was in his stomach. Ashley, seeing what happened, walked over to him, patting his back. His upchucking seemed to have attracted the attention of Cerboura because when he looked up and wiped the puke away from his mouth, the Kaiju was staring at the group of people standing in the street with deadly intent.

Cerboura roared, crashing out of the tangle of buildings he was inside and into the street they were standing on. He roared again at the humans, making them cringe this time. Another defiant and distinctly different roar echoed through the city, making Will spin toward the source. Marugrah charged across the block Cerboura was just in and tackled the bone covered dog-like Kaiju, the two behemoths decimating the next block as they landed. Marugrah bit at the vertebrae-like armor plates on the back of Cerboura's neck. Cerboura's three tails snapped up, the four prongs opening to reveal a red orb in the middle of each of them. The red orbs looked like they were attached more than the creature being born with them. The black orbs lining the sides of the creature's tail also looked like they were attached, lighting up a deep blue color one-by-one from the base of his tail to the pronged end. Yellow streams of lasers erupted from the red orbs, creating a black line in the side of Marugrah's maroon flesh. Marugrah didn't even flinch at the lasers searing into his flesh. He opened his mouth wide and let loose a torrent of green flames upon Cerboura's head. The smaller Kaiju squealed in agony, the flames actually hurting him.

Cerboura's tails wrapped around Marugrah's neck, arm, and snout. The tails pulled on the larger Kaiju, straining to remove the monster off the body they are attached to. Cerboura got his front legs under him and pushed up, Marugrah falling sideways off of him. The ground shook as the massive monster hit the ground, making Will fall on his ass. Cerboura got to his four clawed feet and pounced on Marugrah as he tried to get to his feet himself. Cerboura's weight on his own pushed Marugrah back to the ground. The three-tailed Kaiju clawed at the thick, hard armor plates lining Marugrah's back.

A grenade flew through the air, striking Cerboura in the side. Will looked to see Jones frantically reloading another grenade, her grenade launcher attachment smoking. She was trying to get Cerboura's attention and as Will looked back up to the monster fight, he saw that she had succeeded. Cerboura was staring at the group with evil intent. He hopped down from Marugrah's back, shaking the earth and stalked toward the group, forgetting about his larger opponent.

"Time to go!" Angel said, turning and running the opposite way.

Will stayed locked in place before being pulled away by Ashley. He ran as fast as he could, following the group and feeling the Kaiju gaining on him. Then it all stopped. A whimpering cry sounded out behind him. He glanced back seeing Marugrah grasping at Cerboura's head, pushing his clawed thumbs into the creature's eyes as it cried out in pain. Purple blood gushed from the eye sockets as Marugrah pushed his thumbs deep within them. He had caught Cerboura by surprise, him not seeing the attack coming and now was suffering the consequences of his mistake.

Will turned his eyes forward, tripping over something and tumbling to a stop on his face. He moaned in pain, rolling on his back. He lifted his head up, seeing two Plagueonian ships descend behind Marugrah, firing laser bolts at his neck. Marugrah roared as green blood flew into the air from the laser bolts that hit their mark.

They can be hurt where there is no armor, Will realized.

He turned toward the ships, pulling his thumbs from Cerboura's eye sockets with a sickening slurp. Green fire erupted from his mouth, destroying one of the ships in a ball of yellow flames.

Cerboura groaned with pain as he lifted his head from the ground, sniffing. Without his eyes, he had to rely on his scent. And it must have been good because his eyeless head locked on to Will who was trying to get to his feet, pain racking his body. Cerboura lunged at him, but was stopped as a massive maroon foot slamming atop the Kaiju's head, his jaw breaking audibly, a horrible, gargled screech of agony escaping his throat.

Ashley and Aaron returned, helping Will off the ground.

"Come on, Will. We have to go," Ashley said, supporting his weight.

Will hobbled through the street, his friends keeping him from curling up on the ground in pain, catching up with the rest of the nine-person team.

"Sorry, I tripped," Will wheezed.

"It's alright. We almost did, too," Angel said, looking back at the battle.

Will pushed away from the two people holding on to him, turning to the battle hundreds of feet away… as safe a distance as they could get. Marugrah was lifting Cerboura up by his neck, his sharp obsidian claws digging into the soft flesh and drawing purple blood. He whipped his tail around, driving the clubbed end of his tail into Cerboura's gut, the three spikes on it digging into his flesh as Marugrah repeatedly slammed it into the creature's gut. A piercing gurgling cry erupted from the Kaiju's unhinged and broken jaw that hung limp, saliva and blood flying from his throat with each blow.

Maybe tired of being bullied or wanting to live, Cerboura made a feeble attempt of bringing his three tails up and pounded them against Marugrah's armored back. The effort was all for naught, though. Marugrah slammed the quadruped Kaiju to the ground, grabbed ahold of his limp lower jaw and pulled. The jaw ripped away in a spray of purple blood and a piercing screech of pain. Marugrah grunted in satisfaction, reaching down and grabbing both sides of Cerboura's head. His arms strained as he compressed the monster's head. Cerboura's head exploded in a cloud of purple gore between Marugrah's hands.

Another Kaiju down.

Another one still in Tokyo.

Who-knows-how many to go.

"Damn that was brutal," Aaron remarked.

Seeing that their weapon was dead, the ships flying through the sky suddenly disappeared, teleporting or cloaking themselves as they turned tail and ran. Marugrah threw his head back, roaring in victory. With his job done, he headed back the way he came, heading back to the ocean.

"The Kaiju in Tokyo...it...it just disappeared. It's gone," Boyd's voice reported, sounding stunned.

"Well, where'd it go?" Cole's voice came over Will's earpiece.

"It just disappeared in a flash of bright light."

"Cerboura is dead. Requesting pick up," Angel said into the mic, interrupting their panicking.

"Roger that, Gamma. Request in bound for all fire-teams," Boyd said.

"Roger that, Gamma out."

They may have won two battles, but the war was about to begin, with little chance of winning... and they all knew it.

20

Somewhere above Japan

"My Queen...we have a problem," Tsuzar said, looking at the footage of a Vexnoxtuque that was not Plagueonian-controlled as it drove its clawed thumbs into the Muttorian Vexnoxtuque's eyes.

"What kind of problem?" the Queen asked, sitting on her throne at the back of the ship's massive control room.

Tsuzar transferred the footage to the main screen that also served as the ship's windshield. The fellow Plagueonians in the space gasped as the maroon lizard destroyed one of the transport ships with a blast of green flames.

"What is that beast?" the Queen asked.

"Signatures say it's a Maruian Vexnoxtuque," Tsuzar replied.

"How? All the Maruians we tried to turn into Vexnoxtuque died," the Queen said.

"Unknown... It could be one of the Maruians we followed to this planet," Tsuzar said, watching with awe as the Maruian crushed the Muttorian's head between its hands.

"This thing could jeopardize everything we are working toward on this planet," the Queen growled. "Do we still have no communication with Typhon? We could use the Vexnoxtuque we created for him in this fight. If they are still alive, that is."

"No, my Queen. Still no word from the blood sucker,"

Maloque, a Plagueonian a few stations over said.

"What a shame. Those were some of my favorites. But if he were to have succeeded, this planet would be a wasteland and human free. He was probably killed. The humans have proven themselves quite resourceful. No matter. The remaining creatures under our command should be efficient enough to overwhelm the Maruian and wipe out the mutated apes. Bring the Dagorian back aboard the ship."

"Yes, my Queen," Tsuzar said, working his fingers across his console, activating the teleporter. He locked onto the Dagorian rampaging through the city the humans called Tokyo and teleported the beast back aboard the ship. "It is aboard."

"Good. Now head for the place called...Washington D.C. To rule this planet, we must destroy their most powerful leader. Their...President," the Queen said, a wicked, sharp-toothed smile spread across her face.

"Of course, my Queen," Savernst, the ship's pilot, said.

Their original target was a city called Sydney, Australia, where they would drop another Vexnoxtuque to destroy it, but with the emergence of the Maruian, presumably one of the two that escaped when they plundered Maruia, changed their plans. If they went after the Earth's most powerful leader, the Maruian would surely show up to defend him, and then he would meet his doom.

Tsuzar felt the ship turn, heading for Washington, D.C. They could be there in seconds but that would sink the island of Japan and that wasn't what they wanted. They wanted the world to be rid of humans and to keep the land for themselves so they could build their own cities upon it. A new colony. They had many on their conquered planets, their planet of Hestia having been consumed by a black hole millenia ago. That was what forced them to claim other planets. But the Queen didn't think one planet was sufficient enough.

She needed more.

She made them slaughter millions.

They even made species go extinct, like the Maruians. And the Anterkians. Over a dozen species were extinct because of the Plagueonians. No one questioned the Queen. Except Tsuzar and a few others secretly. They thought the Queen had gone mad. Insane. Especially since she had experimented upon herself with the early Vexnoxtuque serum. She even experimented upon her son, Plague. And after mortally wounded from the battle on Anterkia, she made him into a Vexnoxtuque himself. He was dead now. They had found human footage of his torn open corpse. Only now did they realize the Maruian that killed the Muttorian was the one who must have killed Plague and the advance team. They had scientists aboard the advance team ship along with a Vexnoxtuque making floor. That must have been how the Maruian Vexnoxtuque was made.

Must have been desperate, Tsuzar thought as they sped toward Washington, D.C. where they would arrive in a few hours' time.

He glanced back at the Queen, that wicked smile still on her face. He hated that smile. It was the smile of madness. Of bloodlust. That was what she was. A bloodthirsty monster, just like the creatures they used as weapons. A tyrant, even. That was why nobody

149

questioned her. Her say was like the 'Word of God' to humans.

Yet, he and his followers dared to question her. Not aloud. They'd be executed for that. He had to wait for the right moment to bring her down.

With her death, the Plagueonian race would be free.

With her death, the extinction of entire species would stop.

With her death, the human race would survive.

21

Washington, D.C.

Will fell back on the soft bed of the room he stayed in the night before. The day of fighting monsters and aliens had totally worn him out. He didn't sustain any major injuries but he was in a fair amount of pain. His face was scratched up. His muscles ached. Nothing that won't heal. He wanted to take a shower but couldn't muster the energy to stand from the bed.

His mind wandered into Marugrah's. The behemoth was swimming fast toward Washington, D.C. The Kaiju seemed to not like to be too far away from him. That or something bad was coming to the city. Marugrah was an unnaturally fast swimmer. He swam all the way up the coast in the matter of an hour to save Will and Gamma team from Cerboura. The images of their fight still replayed in his mind. Every grizzly image.

Then there was the matter of all the people killed. All

the people he *saw* be killed. It was enough nightmare fuel for years. Tears started to fill his eyes.

Ashley walked out of the bathroom, climbed on the bed, and on top of Will. She looked into his tear-filled eyes and used her thumbs to wipe the tears from his eyes. She laid her head on his chest and he wrapped his arms around her.

"A lot of people died today," Will said, his voice shaky.

"I know," she said. "And more may die. There is nothing we can do but find a way to stop the Plagueonians and their Kaiju."

"I know. But that won't be easy. We have only gotten this far because Marugrah turned himself into a Kaiju. He is risking himself becoming completely insane for our sake. For humanity. If I could, I'd do the same thing."

Ashley sat up, looking angrily down at Will. "You are not going to become one of those...those things!"

"No, I'm not. But maybe I can do what Marugrah did with Plague. Control a Kaiju and help Marugrah defeat the Plagueonians."

Ashley just stared at him, saying nothing. She rubbed a hand over his stubbled cheek and smiled. Will had no idea what was going through her mind. He had just said he wanted to take over a Kaiju's mind. After what happened to Marugrah, he couldn't imagine what it would do to a human. Maybe she knew she couldn't talk him out of it. Or maybe she just thought he was just spitting out ideas that he'd never follow through with. If that was the case, she was very wrong to assume that.

A knock sounded on the door, making Will groan.

"Who is it?" Ashley asked with a laugh.

"It's me," Nicole's muffled voice from behind the door.

"Me who?" Will asked with a grin.

"Come in," Ashley said, playfully hitting Will in the shoulder.

Nicole walked in wearing sweat pants and a sweat shirt, one of her eyebrows raising as she saw Ashley sitting atop Will.

"What? You don't do this with Jamie?" Will joked.

Nicole's face turned red. "W-what? No!"

Ashley chuckled.

"Don't encourage him," Nicole said, pointing a finger at her as she sat beside them on the bed. "You two have only been together about three days now and you look so in love."

"I wouldn't say 'love'. It's more like taking comfort in each other and trying to keep our minds off of the horrible shit we've been through and seen so far. I'm not saying it's out of the realm of possibility, however," Will said, staring at the ceiling.

"What's up?" Ashley asked, slipping off Will and changing the conversation. Will could tell she was upset about something he just said but didn't know exactly what. It would come up later...maybe.

"I saw you guys in San Francisco. You guys were badass fighting all those aliens," she said, a smile on her face.

"Yeah, well, it wasn't as fun as it looked," Will mumbled.

"I'm sure it wasn't. That is not what I'm saying."

"Then what are you saying, then?"

"I'm saying that it was brave of you three to go out there and do something I couldn't for the greater good."

Will sat up with a groan and pulled Nicole in a hug. She hugged back. "It's alright you didn't go. It isn't something everyone can do."

"He's right. We were scared shitless but we still got it done. To be honest, if Marugrah didn't show up, we probably would have been Kaiju kibble," Ashley said.

"Yeah, but you guys handled it well," Nicole said as they pulled away from each other.

Will and Ashley smiled at each other, Nicole's words making them feel a little better after the horrors they just endured.

Nicole hopped to her feet, her hands behind her back. "Dinner is about done. You two are coming, right?"

"Yeah, of course," Ashley said.

Will's stomach rumbled loudly. "I guess I am, too."

He rolled off the bed, dropping to the floor. His body ached, but like any living thing, he needed food. He followed Nicole out of the room, Ashley right behind him.

"Marudon having any luck tracking the Plagueonian Mothership?" he asked as they stepped onto the elevator that would take them to the mess hall on the second floor.

"Not that I've heard. She finished the device a few hours ago but they can't exactly get it to work. She's working on it, though," Nicole explained as the elevator descended.

There was a moment of silence before the doors opened, the sounds of echoing conversations, most of them solemn in tone, flooding Will's ears. There were less people than Will imagined there would be. Some of the fire-team soldiers must've died in the San Francisco battle is all he could figure. It was a horrible battle, after all.

Nicole led them to a table on the far corner of the mess hall where Aaron, Jamie, and Walt were already sitting, eating and laughing. Three waiting plates of steaming hot food sat in front of empty spots. Nicole sat by Jamie and Walt on one side of the table while Will and Ashley sat next to Aaron on the other.

"All the heroes are together," Jamie said with a beaming smile.

"You wanna get laid, you gotta fight some aliens and almost get munched by a giant monster," Aaron said, a sly grin aimed at Jamie.

"Oh, shut up man. I don't see any chicks swarming all over you," Jamie said, waving him off.

"They will soon enough!" Aaron countered.

Will dug into his food: a hamburger, french fries, and a Mountain Dew. He took a big bite from the burger, then cracked open the Mountain Dew and took a long gulp of it, washing down the burger. When he looked back to the rest of the group, they were staring at him.

"What?" he asked, him mouth full of food.

"You alright, dude?" Walt asked.

"I'm just...hungry. Really, really hungry..."

His mind slipped from his body and into the mind of the giant Kaiju lurking in the ocean off of Florida, consuming whales, fish, sharks, anything to satiate his growing hunger. A hunger Will had seen in Cerboura as he consumed the people of San Francisco. He took pleasure in it. Marugrah didn't want to become that.

Will didn't want Marugrah to become that: a ravenous monster that only wanted to devour and destroy.

His mind returned to his own body, hearing his name being called over and over again as someone tried to get his attention.

"Huh, what?" he said, a little dazed.

"You spaced out...again," Ashley said, a concerned hand on his shoulder.

"I...can't control when it happens. It just...happens," Will said, rubbing his eyes. The mental connection to Marugrah was quite frustrating, almost getting him killed once already. Maybe it could be useful in the future though? Maybe he could find a way to communicate with the creature? All he had was maybes, though.

"I'm sure you'll be able to soon enough. You'll figure it out," Walt said with a smile.

"Yeah, I hope so. Otherwise it's going to get me killed, especially if it happens while we're in the middle of a battle."

They continued their meal, listening to Aaron's stories about the battle in San Francisco and stories he thought were funny. A few actually made Will laugh despite his foul mood which seemed to lighten up, forgetting about the death and destruction he had witnessed.

Until a voice came over the intercom saying, "Gamma squad report to the control room, ASAP. All other fire-teams standby for further orders."

"Well, that was nice while it lasted," Ashley grumbled, standing from the table.

"All work and no play, it seems," Aaron said, standing as well.

Will stood, saying nothing. He knew if they were calling them to the control room, they had found something. Either Wraith or a new Kaiju had shown up or they found the mothership. He followed Ashley and Aaron to the elevator, taking it to the top floor. It opened and they walked out, down the hall, and into the control room.

As they entered the control room, Will gasped. The screen at the front of the room showed a marker moving through West Virginia toward Washington, D.C. in Maryland on a detailed map of the United States.

Cole, Marudon, and the soldiers of Gamma squad turned toward the sound of Will's gasp.

"Ah, Will. There you are," Cole said.

"Marudon's device works, I see. A bit late, by the looks of it. They're almost here," Will commented as he stared at the screen.

"That was what we were just discussing. We are about to mobilize troops and have alerted the President."

"That is who they are after."

"The President?"

Cole looked stunned as if this information was new to him. Marudon must not have known that was their target or just didn't tell him.

"Yeah. That was who Plague was coming after. The President is the most powerful leader on earth. That will be their first target. Once he's dead, they will move onto the leaders of other countries before destroying their citizens," Will explained.

"If that's true, we need extra security around the White House or get the President out of D.C.," Cole said, trying to formulate a plan.

"With all due respect, sir, if we try to put the President onto Air Force One, it will be shot out of the sky. It's already too late to try and get him out of the city by car," Angel said.

"You're right. Fine. I have no choice then. I am putting your team in charge of his protection."

"Excuse me, sir?"

"Every other team is broken and incomplete. Your team is the only intact team. Today's battle with Cerboura and the Plagueonian forces in San Francisco has severely diminished our forces. Your team seems to be the most capable at the moment. All of our forces will be there to back you up. Let's hope Marugrah will be there to help us defend the capital from the coming Kaiju assault."

"He'll be here," Will said, confident in his friend's abilities.

The icon on the screen was now on the edge of Maryland. It would be there very soon.

"Alright. Go. Get ready. You have to be at the White House by the time that ship arrives. I'll call now and inform him on the situation," Cole said frantically.

Gamma squad rushed out of the control room, Will, Ashley, and Aaron following them. They squeezed into the elevator, taking it down to the armory. They quickly dressed themselves in body armor and procured their weaponry that they used in the San Francisco battle.

"Twice in one day," Will mumbled, looking over his M4 carbine.

"You'll get used to it," Walker said, talking from experience. He looked like he had been in many battles. "You ready to save the President?"

"As ready as I will ever be."

22

"What are you talking about?" John Scott, the President of the United States of America, asked into the phone as he sat behind the Resolute desk.

"I'm talking about the shit storm that happened in New York City, San Francisco, and Tokyo is about to land on our doorstep here in D.C., sir. The alien race responsible for the attacks on our cities has set their cross-hairs on you," the man on the phone said, who Scott knew was the Creature Counter Unit Director Lance Cole. "I've sent a team of my best soldiers to come and aid in yours and the White House's protection. They should be there very soon."

"And why am I not able to get out of the city before the shit storm starts? Wouldn't that be the logical thing to do instead of assigning more people to my security detail?"

"The ship will shoot any aircraft out of the sky. If you try to get out by car, you will be trampled by a Kaiju or Kaijus or be assaulted by Plagueonian ground forces. Trust me, sir, you will be safer in the White House. We'll do our best to evacuate civilians."

"I hope you're right, Cole. If this goes sideways, your ass is out of a job."

"If this goes sideways, we may not live long enough for you to fire me." Cole hung up on him.

He looked at the phone a moment before hanging it

up. He had seen what Cole had done to try to stop the Kaijus that attacked New York City and San Francisco without his permission, having bypassed the normal bureaucracy of government decisions for military action.

Maybe I gave the CCU too much power, he thought.

The decimated cities will take decades to rebuild because of Cole's drastic stunts of dropping MOABs on alien monsters. The only way he had seen them being killed was by another creature. One that he claims to be on their side. Cole must have faith that the red dragon would show up. Marugrah, Scott believed the monster's name was.

He looked around the Oval Office. In front of the ornately carved Resolute desk were two flower print couches facing each other. The gold and white oval rug that covered most of the floor had a weird but modern design that Scott couldn't make heads or tails of. What he did recognize were the red flowers covering the design.

He stood from the desk as four Secret Service agents rushed in, eight more soldiers entering behind them. He looked at the eight CCU soldiers, three of them looking too young to even be armed the way they are and the other five looked like battle hardened veterans.

"So, you are the soldiers here to protect me?" Scott asked.

"Yes, sir. Gamma squad at your service," the woman with short blond hair said with a salute.

"At ease, soldier. When are these so-called aliens supposed to make landfall here?"

"Approximately..."

Sirens started to wail in the distance.

"...now."

"You four..." Scott pointed to the Secret Service men, "...get everyone you can out of the White House. The Vice President, Chief of Staff, my wife, my daughter. Everyone. I want them out of the city before those hell-beasts reach us."

The men looked unsure, but he pointed forcefully at the door they came through with a stern look and they complied.

"Eva, you stay with the President," the short-haired woman said to another female soldier holding a giant sniper rifle.

The woman known as 'Eva' moved deeper into the room, standing beside Scott who stood behind his desk. The younger soldier wearing a beanie cap shifted uncomfortably, as if he didn't like the decision or wanted to stay himself. None of the other soldiers noticed as it was a light gesture, but Scott's keen eyes caught the move.

At least he thought so until the short-haired woman said, "Charming, you too."

The young man known as...'Charming' rolled his eyes and said, "I really hate that callsign."

Scott agreed. It was a stupid callsign for a soldier but maybe it held some meaning he didn't understand.

The remaining six CCU soldiers rushed out of the Oval Office, leaving Scott alone with two armed guards and potentially a coming horde of monsters wanting nothing more than to see him dead.

Will followed the soldiers of Gamma squad out of the Oval Office and through the White House. He had never been in the White House before but didn't have time for a tour. They hurried through the building, everything passing by him in a blur, soon coming upon an elevator. They crammed in it, riding up. Will didn't know if it led to the roof but he'd soon find out.

The doors opened, vomiting them into the hallway beyond which was black besides the red emergency lights along the ceiling that granted them a little bit of sight. They hurried down the long hallway to a short staircase leading to a solid-looking door with a numeric keypad and a hand print security system. The Secret Service Agent removed the black glove from his hand and placed it on the scanner before typing in a code on the keypad. He opened the door, cool night air surging into the hallway along with the sounds of screams and screeching car tires mixed with emergency vehicle sirens. The air raid sirens still wailed but were far off in the distance.

They stepped onto the White House roof. Will was awed at the drastic transformation that took place from when he first entered the building to now. Chain guns lined the roof walls, two to the north, two to the south. What looked like air conditioning vents had tranformed into missile launchers controlled from inside the security room, buried several levels below where he stood. Secret Service Agents and regular soldiers armed with grenade launchers and high caliber rifles lined the roof as well.

The roar of a distant Kaiju echoed through the city, making the human screams grow louder as they struggled to get out of the city. Will made his way to the edge of the roof in time to see cars speed away out of the driveway around the South Lawn. They probably contained the President's family and some of Washington's most important people just as President Scott had ordered the Secret Service Agents to do.

They'd probably fly people out but didn't want to chance a Plagueonian ship being cloaked nearby and shooting them out of the sky. Will knew the President would flee if he could. But there was nowhere to go without the aliens following. Their only chance was to stop them right here and now. He knew a lot of people would die in the coming battle. The coming...war. But that was what happened in war, right? People fought. People died.

It wasn't like this, though.

In human wars, no one had Kaijus as weapons.

Will looked into the distance, trying to spot the coming monster but instead saw a ship. The giant Plagueonian mothership hovered above the city miles away but still looked massive. Hundreds of smaller ships erupted from hatches in the grey ship's hull. Most of them heading toward the White House.

The battle for Earth was about to begin.

162

HUMANITY'S LAST STAND

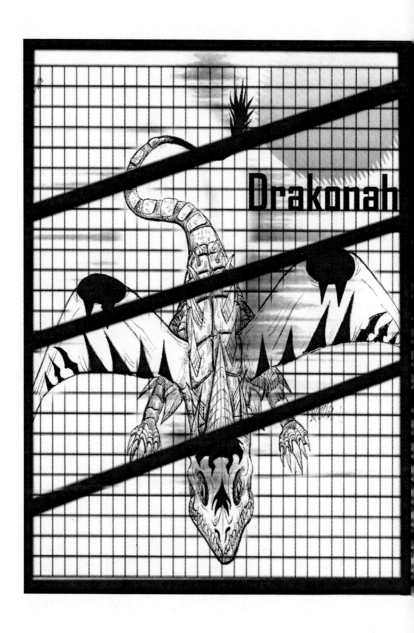

23

Marugrah rose from Chesapeake Bay, sea water draining from the crags and folds in his maroon, armored hide. He waded through the bay toward Chesapeake Beach, doing his best to not crush the homes of the people living there as he surfaced on dry land. He passed through a wooded area, following it until Andrew's Air Force Base where he charged across the large field that jets took off from and through Morningside, where he was unable to avoid crushing homes and the people within them that had not been evacuated yet. He charged through homes and small buildings as he made his way into the city of Washington D.C., America's capital. He looked ahead, seeing The large Plagueonian mothership sitting in the sky, smaller ships flocking to where he knew the White House was located, a Kaiju covered in tentacles and armor crawling out of the Tidal Basin and making its way to the White House as well.

He sensed four other Kaiju in the city as well. He looked around, spotting them. All four were converging on the White House. He increased his speed, running at the tentacle monster which was the closest. The other three were farther into the city, coming from behind the White House. Within a few minutes he was behind the monster, grabbing at its armored back. The creature screeched in surprise, not hearing or noticing his approach.

More tentacles sprang from under Wraith's overlapping armor plates along her back and wrapped around Marugrah's neck and arms. He roared in frustration as the tentacles wrapped around his body pushed him to the ground. The white hide of Wraith's body seemingly sparked, electricity streaking down the tentacles, shooting into his body. Marugrah let out a high-pitched shriek before letting loose a stream of green flames, severing the eight tentacles protruding from the monster's back.

Wraith let out a pained roar of her own, backpedaling on her eight legs, just feet from the Washington Monument (the tallest obelisk in the world, standing at 555 feet). To Marugrah's astonishment, the tentacles he severed began to regenerate before his eyes. Wraith's mandibles twitched with agitation as she ran at him, head lowered and ready to ram him with her armored noggin. Marugrah swung around, dragging his club tipped tail which smacked into the charging Kaiju's side and threw it to the ground, crushing the National World War II Memorial under her mass.

He took a step toward the fallen white spider-like creature but didn't get any farther. Something big collided with his side, felling him to the ground just feet from the United States Holocaust Memorial Museum. He rolled to his feet as fast as he could with his bulk. Once he was up, he came face-to-face with a bluish-green dragonfly-like monster hovering in the air, its wings flapping rapidly to keep its mass aloft. Its face frozen in a permanent sneer, its curved sharp teeth showing. Eight blazing red eyes stared hungrily at him. Mandibles jutting from the side of its face twitch with anticipation. Its back was lined with overlapping plates of armor. A tail swung down toward the ground, tipped with a wicked looking stinger. Its eight legs lining the creature's sides twitched as well.

It barked a challenge, begging Marugrah to fight it.

He complied.

Will watched as Marugrah charged at the new Kaiju that looked like a giant, armored dragonfly. The crazed creature seemed delighted as it rose up and dove at Marugrah. The two giants collided, clawing and biting each other in a ferocious clash. Wraith just seemed to watch the fight with amusement. Until she charged, wanting to join in on the action.

"Incoming!" somebody yelled, pulling Will away from the unfair battle of giants.

Will's eyes snapped to the South Lawn where an army of Plagueonians ran toward the White House from a ship that made it past the House's missile defense systems. The roof's chain guns fired into the mass of armored invaders. The Secret Service Agents and soldiers did as well, along with the soldiers of Gamma squad, Will and his friends included.

Aliens fell dead on the lawn, but more seemed to take their place. Before Will knew it, there were two more ships dropping alien soldiers onto the South Lawn. A shadow fell over the White House making everyone on its roof spin toward the North Lawn where another Kaiju stood.

Will thought it looked bird-like or even dragon-like. Dragon-like not like Marugrah was, but more like a wyvern-type dragon. Its face looked like the skull of a dragon, its wings being folded at its sides, a giant claw protruding from the tips of the wings. Black markings covered the Kaiju's dark blue flesh. Its neck was covered in overlapping rings of armor. Armor plates ran down the creature's chest and stomach. Some sort of carapace ran down the monster's spine, two rows of jagged spikes protruding from the carapace. Its legs were heavily armored, a spike protruding from its knee, the limb ending in four, claw tipped digits. A tail twitched behind it, segments of the carapace lining it. It ended in a bundle of spikes.

The creature looked at the men on the roof for a moment before extending its wings. Will didn't think they were big enough to lift the monster's mass off of the ground...until they expanded. The chicken-like wings turned into giant hawk-like wings, minus the feathers. It squawked and flapped the giant, five-hundred-foot wing-span wings. Once it was high enough in the air, it glided over the White House and toward the battle raging between Marugrah, Wraith, and the dragonfly Kaiju.

Zorax, Will thought, giving the giant bug a name. He didn't know why he liked the name, or how his mind fit them together. It just sounded cool and alien at the same time. As for the giant bird...

Drakonah, he decided. The name coming to him after a phrase he learned a long time ago, *kranio drakos*, keeping the *drako* part and adding a *nah* to the end. The phrase meant 'skull dragon' in, like, Greek or something. He couldn't remember. He knew parts of a few languages, mostly learning them out of sheer boredom.

Marugrah doesn't stand a chance against three Kaijus, Will thought, looking out at the battle Drakonah was heading toward.

"ETA on that package I ordered?" Will asked,

toggling his throat mic. "Maru won't stand a chance against Wraith, Zorax, *and* Drakonah."

"Zorax? Drakonah?" Cole's voice came through his earpiece.

"The dragonfly and the bird-dragon Kaijus."

"Copy that. Package should be there now. What about the giant, walking plant?"

The what? Will thought, spinning toward the North Lawn Drakonah was just a moment before. The creature Cole asked about was trudging toward the White House on four stocky legs, looking as if they were composed of bundles of vines. Red rose pedals framed the Kaiju's thorn covered head. Three long tendrils covered in bumps extend from the monster's side.

"Shit!" he yelled, alerting anyone nearby to the creature's approach.

Soldiers and Secret Service Agents turned and fired at the new beast. It let out a wailing warble, the proximity shaking Will's insides and making him cringe in pain from the sound being so loud. The soldiers and agents firing were somehow able to keep firing at the beast, not that they were able to hurt it.

The Kaiju had no eyes that Will could see, but it was seemingly glaring at the men and women on the roof. It didn't make a move and Will took the time to figure out a good name for the monster.

"Vishlari," Will finally said.

"What the hell kind of name is that?" Cole asked.

"*Ko'p tishlari*. It's the Uzbek word for *'many teeth'*. I just took that and added a *v* instead of the *ko'p* and the *t* 'cause it sounds cool and it kinda looks like it has a venus fly trap for a head. Vishlari."

"How do you know Uzbek?"

"I got bored a lo... oh shit."

One of Vishlari's six tendrils hit the White House roof where Will had been standing a moment before. If he hadn't dived to the side, he would have been turned into a crimson pancake on the roof. A few Secret Service Agents and soldiers weren't as lucky, however.

Will half expected the blow to decimate the building, but the Kaiju must have been holding back. The roof was cracked from where the tendril hit but there was no further damage. He looked around the roof for his team, finding them still firing into the horde of aliens storming across the South Lawn.

Minus Ashley.

Will started to panic for until he spotted her at the door they entered the roof at with the package he ordered.

A FGM-148 Javelin rocket launcher with the special CCU rocket containing the mind control doohickey.

On the way to the White House, Will had asked Cole to have it delivered as he didn't have time to ask him about it before they left the CCU HQ. Cole didn't question the idea. He knew what Will planned to do with it. And he had the perfect target in mind.

Drakonah.

The back of the Kaiju's head wasn't armored.

While Vishlari didn't look armored the way the other Kaiju were, he knew the vine-looking skin was the actual armor. And that covered the monster from head-to-toe. And Wraith's neck and head were heavily armored.

Drakonah was the logical choice.

Will rushed over to her and took the launcher from

her.

"You sure this is gonna work? Marugrah didn't have much luck with Plague," she said to him.

"Yeah, well, I'm not Maru and this beast isn't Plague," Will said, affixing the obsidian metal headband atop his head.

"Just so you know, if you're thrown out of the creature's head and become brain dead, I'm not going to be giving you sponge baths and feeding you chocolate pudding," she smirked as Will aimed the launcher at the battle between Marugrah and the three alien Kaiju.

Zorax jabbed her stinger into Marugrah's unarmored side as he was being held by Wraith's tentacles protruding from her back, eliciting a wail of pain from the reptilian behemoth. Drakonah watched the battle, her back to the White House.

And Will.

He locked onto the back of Drakonah's head, between her skull-like head and the carapace lining her back, aiming for the soft flesh in between.

"I doubt that," Will said with a smirk of his own and pulled the trigger.

24

"You think they're actually going be able to stop those things?" Scott asked, irking Eva.

She wanted to release a string of curses at the man for doubting her teammates but held her tongue as he was the President of the United States of America.

Something about the man just rubbed her the wrong way.

Probably his lack of being able to do his job, Eva thought, recalling all the failed missions she ran that were ordered by the man quaking behind the Resolute desk.

"If anyone can do it, it's the man mentally linked to our very own Godzilla," Charming said, a smile on his face.

Eva nodded. He was right. Will was the only one that held any real chance at helping humanity prevail against their current enemy.

He had a plan.

The building shook from an impact to the roof. Eva looked up, almost expected to see a Kaiju's face burrow through the roof to get at the President. She didn't doubt that the beasts would do it.

A smaller bang from the one on the roof turned their attention toward the Oval Office's door.

Something -or *somethings*- had made it into the White House.

Eva took aim with her Barrett M82 sniper rifle, waiting for the door to open and a horde of alien monsters to swarm in.

Five minutes passed and no creatures came. It was quiet besides the roars of the distant Kaijus and the gunfire coming from the roof. She glanced at Charming, the same confused look on his face. She looked at Scott who just looked scared shitless. Eva found it a tiny bit funny but she was actually just as scared. She had served three tours in Iraq. She was used to a human enemy, not technologically advanced aliens.

These creatures were worse than humans.

The door burst open, a roaring Plagueonian standing in the doorway, raising his weapon toward the three people in the room. Scott let out a squeal of fright and ducked down behind the Resolute desk as Eva fired and took the monster's head off in a cloud of purple gore.

Three more entered the room, firing laser bolts from their weapons. Eva took cover behind the flower print couch they moved to either side of the Resolute desk. Charming did the same. The smell of burning fabric filled the room as the bolts hit the couches, but, luckily, didn't punch through them.

Gunfire filled the space as Charming sprang up and fired at the aliens with his SCAR, felling two of them, while Eva dropped the third.

But there were already more.

One of the four newcomers fired their weapon, Eva barely dodging the shot. She landed on the ground, pulling the trigger on her sniper, punching a hole through the creature's chest armor. Charming fired a few shots, killing another. She aimed at the third one, shot, and missed. The Plagueonian seemed to anticipate the shot and dodged it. It wasn't able to dodge Charming's, however.

Bullets enter the side of its exposed face, taking off its non-existent nose and its upper lip area. The alien soldier turned its mangled face toward its attacker, getting riddled with more of Charming's bullets. The alien dropped dead in a puddle of its own blood.

The remaining alien standing in the doorway brought its weapon up toward Charming when some sort of blade erupted from its chest. The creature looked stunned as it slowly turned its head down to look at the hole in its chest. A laser bolt blew apart its head, making the alien's body fall forward to reveal another Plagueonian holding a smoking laser rifle in one hand and a sword with a blade made of crackling energy in the other.

What the hell? Eva thought, confused as to why a Plagueonian would kill one of their own.

Eva aimed her rifle at the creature, but didn't fire. Charming followed her lead.

"Don't shoot. I have come to help," the creature said, holding up its arms.

"And why the hell would we believe that? Your friends just tried to kill us. This could all just be some elaborate ploy to get close to us before killing us," Charming said, actually making sense to Eva.

"Well, I did just kill one of my own. Even if he was misguided, it's not a pleasurable thing to do. And we Plagueonians would never do such a thing as that. We would just kill you outright."

"Misguided?" Eva asked.

"Yes. They follow the Queen, whose views are not to my liking. Others feel the same way. We want to stop her. To keep her from enslaving or wiping anymore species out of existence. Many have fallen because of the Queen's madness. We want to stop it. Here and now."

"As do we. We don't want to die. But how do we know we can trust you and what you say?"

"I suppose you can't. You're just going to have to."

Eva thought on it, her rifle still aimed at the creature.

"Fine," she finally said, lowering her weapon. "Where

are these others you are talking about?"

25

"Who are you?" a voice asked in the darkness that surrounded him. It was everywhere he turned. He couldn't see anything but the darkness.

"I am... William Carver....Human," Will said, trying to see something. Anything. But there was only darkness. Cold, empty darkness.

Is this the mind of a Kaiju? Will wondered.

"No. This is the part of my mind that was locked away long ago. The only part of me that has not been driven mad when I was turned into this grotesque monster," the voice said, answering his mental question.

Will concluded that thinking was the same as talking while connected to a Kaiju mind.

"So, you're not all the way...an evil killing machine?" Will asked.

"No. I am not. But I can't control my actions. My body forces me to kill. To *devour*."

"I understand. None of you wanted to become...monsters."

"Why are you here, human?"

"To help my friend...my friends. My species."

"How do you plan to do that?"

"By...controlling you. Fighting the other Kaijus. Destroying the Plagueonian armada...somehow."

"Are you sure that is a wise idea? Entering a

Vexnoxtuque mind will put yours in jeopardy. You could become just as insane as the creature you overtake."

"It's a risk I'm willing to take. For my friends. For my *planet*."

A figure emerged from the darkness. In ways, it was closely related to how Marugrah looked before he turned himself into a Kaiju, lacking any of the armor and horrifying features. It stood as tall as Will, with the same skull-like head the creature's Kaiju form did and looked pretty much the same, too. It had arms instead of wings that ended in three clawed fingers. Its tail was long and thin, not having the bundle of spines at the end. Its legs were the same as her Kaiju form but with none of the armor. Its skin was smooth and blue in color. Its body was curvy, like a woman's. Definitely a girl. Now that he thought about it, the creature's voice also sounded feminine.

"I admire what you are willing to do for the ones you love. If it is control you want, then have it. Have me do something good after so long of evil deeds," she said.

Will's vision faded to black, erasing the creature and replacing it with a stretch of grass and curved roads leading to the base of the Washington Monument. He felt the ground beneath him, realizing he was lying on his side. The roars of Marugrah, Zorax, and Wraith filled his ears.

He rolled on his stomach, trying to get his arms under him but they didn't feel right. Then he remembered he was in Drakonah's body. She didn't have arms. She had wings. So he tried another tactic. He got Drakonah's legs under her body and lifted, the powerful legs lifting her massive weight.

He almost fell back down once he was up. The Kaiju's four-hundred-foot height was dizzying. So dizzying that it made him -Drakonah- pitch forward and heaved whatever contents were in the monster's stomach onto the grass and roads below the creature. Some sort of black goo mixed with the corpses of people spilled out of Drakonah's mouth. Will could taste the vile-stew as it came out of the creature's massive maw. He Kaiju-vomited again, propelled by disgust this time until there was nothing left in the monster's stomach.

I share your disgust, the female voice said. *But do not forget your task.*

Right, he thought, looking to the battle between the giants.

Wraith clung to Marugrah's armored back with her eight spider-like legs, her tentacles sending sparks of electricity into his body. Zorax just watched with amusement, taking pleasure in the saurian Kaiju's pain, clapping her front two legs that ended in pincers together.

The sight pissed Will off.

He forgot about his disgust and charged the flying monster, Zorax seeing him coming, confusion in her eyes. And then malice. Will jumped at Zorax, flapping Drakonah's wings wildly and extending her legs forward, claws ready to tear her apart, but he missed. Zorax dove to the side, avoiding his strike. Will landed where Zorax was, the ground crumbling beneath Drakonah's mass.

Searing pain radiated from Drakonah's side, making Will cry out, the sound coming out as a high-pitched roar. He looked down, seeing Zorax's massive stinger embedded in Drakonah's side. Before the giant dragonfly could retract her stinger, Will lunged down and bit down on Zorax's tail. She wailed in pain as he dug Drakonah's sharp teeth deeper into the Kaiju-insect's flesh. Will could feel Zorax's hot blood filling Drakonah's mouth, tasting the nasty metallic liquid.

Zorax stabbed at the back of Drakonah's neck with her blade-like pincers, Will feeling each blow as the pincers tore apart Drakonah's flesh, but rage came with each attack. Rage was what motivated the Kaijus. Rage and hunger. The rage allowed Will to move past the pain and do what he did next. He willed Drakonah's head to thrash back and forth like a dog, shredding the flesh of Zorax's tail, purple blood spraying in all directions.

The stinger slipped from Drakonah's side with a slurp and a geyser of purple blood. Zorax was able to get out of the death grip Will had on her tail, a chunk of flesh now missing from it. He spat it out, it landing with a splat on the ground. The action sent Zorax into some sort of anger-filled frenzy. She dove at him, colliding with Drakonah's armored chest and wrapping her eight legs around the bird Kaiju's body, digging her claws into her sides. Zorax's wings flapped harder, lifting Drakonah off the ground.

Holy shit, these things are strong! Will thought as Zorax carried Drakonah into the city.

He stretched out Drakonah's wings and drove the sharp talons at the end into the insect Kaiju's side. Zorax's legs let go of Drakonah with a high-pitched shriek. Drakonah landed on the Verizon Center, squashing it and the surrounding buildings beneath her massive weight. Will rolled to Drakonah's feet. As soon as he was up, he was hit from behind and knocked to the ground again.

Will felt Zorax's stinger stab into Drakonah's back, something spurting from the stinger and into the bird-Kaiju's veins. Venom maybe? Will it kill Drakonah and leave Marugrah to fight three Kaijus on his own?

Fear not, human. The Vexnoxtuque's venom will have no effect on me. This isn't the first time it stung me, the mysterious female voice said. *I was not a willing participant in their experiments*, the voice informed him.

Knowing that the venom will do nothing to Drakonah, he instructed her to get to her feet and whirled on the giant bug, lunging forward and plunging the spikes at the end of Drakonah's wings into Zorax's flapping wings. The flapping stopped, the creature only hovering over the ground because Will was holding the creature by her impaled wings. He threw Zorax to the ground, squishing Mount Vernon Square.

He stomped on the creature's head a few times with Drakonah's clawed feet before being stopped by a pained wail. He looked to see that Vishlari had decided to join the fight against Marugrah. He snapped his six tendrils, which were now covered in spikes, at Marugrah who was still struggling to dislodge Wraith from his back. He must not have seen the battle between Drakonah and Zorax because when Will had her sprint across the city and tackle the plant-monster, he was completely caught off guard.

The two giants fell into the Washington Monument which shook violently, but, incredibly, still stayed standing. Will caught a glimpse of Marugrah as he flung Wraith off of him and charged her. Vishlari hissed menacingly at Drakonah who roared back just as menacingly before biting off one of the plant-Kaiju's six tendril arms in a spray of purple blood. Vishlari roared in pain and wrapped his remaining tendrils around Drakonah's body, the spikes covering them digging into her armored skin. The anger and hatred flowing through Drakonah's body countered the searing pain of the spikes in her flesh, allowing Will to repeatedly bite at the creature's neck.

But Vishlari seemed to know Drakonah was going to try that and wrapped one of his spike-laden tendrils around her snout. Will, lost in the rage that fuels Drakonah, kept trying to open the bird-monster's mouth, shaking her head to try to dislodge the tendril, but the spikes covering it kept it in place. While Will thrashed Drakonah about, Vishlari was able to push her off of him and throw her to the ground.

You are losing yourself, human, the female voice came again. *Control the rage. Don't let it consume you. Otherwise, you will be stuck in this body forever.*

Control the rage, he thought.

Will snarled at Vishlari so angrily, the Kaiju looked taken aback a little by the display of aggression. He got Drakonah's wings under Vishlari and plunged the spikes at the end into his chest, the claws slipping through Vishlari's vine-like armor easily. Will hoped they struck some vital organs on their way through.

Unfortunately, that wasn't the case. Vishlari did squeal in pain, but the creature quickly turned its flower petal frilled, eyeless head back to Drakonah who was still laying on her back. He opened his mouth full of hundreds of sharp teeth wide and lunged down, meaning to engulf Drakonah's head and rip it off. Without Will even thinking, Drakonah's mouth snapped open, a rainbow of color exploding from her gullet. The ray of concentrated light shot into Vishlari's mouth and exploded out the monster's back in a spray of green flesh and purple blood.

Vishlari stumbled back, knocking into the Washington Monument again which swayed but still did not fall over...until Wraith crashed into the opposite side of the Monument. The base of the obelisk of untold historical value crumbled and fell to the ground, crushing the already dying Vishlari.

One more to go, Will thought as he got to Drakonah's feet.

Will turned his attention to Wraith who was pushing herself back onto her eight legs, using the tentacles on her back to push herself up. He took a step forward, a searing pain radiating from Drakonah's lower back, seeping through the rage. Will craned Drakonah's head down, seeing the tip of a giant stinger protruding from her armor plated gut.

What the hell? Will thought, confused.

He looked back, seeing the snarling face that he thought he smashed in.

Zorax was still alive.

And pissed.

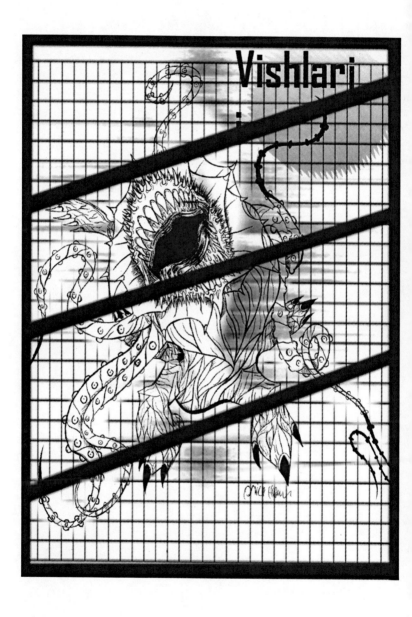

Vishlari

26

The armor on Zorax's face was cracked and leaking purple blood, but she otherwise seemed fine. She retracted her stinger from Drakonah's back sending blinding pain throughout her body. Will whirled on the bug Kaiju, but the movement made the pain unbearable and Drakonah pitched forward, holding her stomach in a human gesture of pain. Zorax let out a few grunts that could have been laughter. Drakonah snapped up her own tail, unleashing a barrage of spikes from the tip at the sadistic beast. With a quickness Will wasn't expecting, Zorax dove to the side, dodging the launched spikes.

The rage returned from Will not hitting his target, allowing him to stand Drakonah up straight and aim better. Zorax flew over the crumbled ruins of the Washington Monument and the crushed body of Vishlari, around the base of the Monument, and toward the battle between Marugrah and Wraith in an effort to avoid the firing spikes. Fortunately, Wraith was in front of Marugrah, the spikes ricocheting off of her armored carapace, but made her turn toward Drakonah. Will stopped firing spikes, knowing he had just pissed off the beast.

Marugrah had other plans, however.

With her back to Marugrah, Wraith didn't see the coming attack. He opened his mouth, unleashing a torrent of fire upon her armored back. At first, she didn't react. When she did, it was a high pitched roar of anger and pain mixed together.

Zorax came out of nowhere, ramming Marugrah and

knocking him to the ground. Wraith, no longer being assaulted by Marugrah's flames, pounced on him, her armored back smoldering. While Will's attention was on the battle between Marugrah and Wraith, Zorax saw the opportunity to attack. She did the same thing she did with Marugrah, knocking down Drakonah and then jabbing her claws into Drakonah's armored chest with a quickness and ferocity that surprised Will.

Will raised Drakonah's wings in front of her body, trying to avoid more damage to her vital parts but in the process getting her wings torn to shreds. He got Drakonah's legs under Zorax and pushed. Zorax flew through the air, landing on her back hundreds of feet away, crushing the National Aquarium. She bucked and squirmed but was unable to get up and then fell still.

Will took a step toward the creature, then another, each time feeling the life draining from Drakonah.

Time to go, human, the mysterious voice said. *But before you do, I will instill you with a gift.*

Will's mind flooded with images. Monsters like the ones he had seen the last few days. Ancient Greece being devastated. A war between monsters. And as quickly as they came, they were gone and he felt himself lying on his back.

He opened his eyes slowly, feeling disoriented from the shift in minds. He now knew who Drakonah was before she was turned into a Kaiju. Dal-Un was her name. The last Anterkian. She traveled here with her Guardian. The images of the Guardian were fuzzy and unclear to him.

Once his vision focused, he was looking into the face of Ashley who looked relieved. He smiled at her and she helped him up. He almost hurled, the switch from being four-hundred-feet tall to six-feet being just as disorienting as the opposite was. He composed himself and looked around.

The sight he saw made him reach for his M4 but found it gone. He reached for the pistol holstered on his leg but was stopped by Ashley.

"Will, wait!" she yelled, grabbing his forearm and stopping him from grabbing the gun just inches from his hand.

Will gave her a questioning look.

"A lot has happened while you were away," she told him.

He looked back to the scene on the roof. The Secret Service Agents and soldiers on the roof looked uncomfortable about their presence. Even President Scott looked uncomfortable. Plagueonians. About ten of them stood on the roof among the human forces that were there when he entered Drakonah's head. Something was different about them, though. They didn't give off a threatening vibe to him like the others he had fought so far.

"A lot as in...?" Will asked, raising a questioning eyebrow at her.

"Well, for starters, we have made some friends." Aaron said, walking up beside Will. "Nice job out there. That was really friggin' awesome."

"Yeah, well, I had some help. So, what? We have Plagueonians on our side now?"

"Yep. They got tired of their Queen's shit and are going to help us take her down. They even have a few ships to help us get there."

Will just grunted, looking out at the battle between Marugrah and Wraith. The two behemoths charged at each other, Wraith snapping the tentacles on her back at Marugrah, electricity sparking on his hide each time they made contact, Marugrah roaring in pain.

The forms of Vishlari, Drakonah, and Zorax lay motionless. Dead. Or so Will hoped.

The chops of helicopters and the whines of jets turned everyone's eyes to the sky. A-10 Thunderbolts, F-22 Raptors, Black Hawks and AH-64 Apaches charged through the sky toward the battling monsters.

"Cole must've ordered an attack," Ashley observed.

"I hope he told them not to attack Marugrah," Will muttered.

Will's head snapped to the side as Angel approached with a Plagueonian at her side.

"Welcome back to the real world, William. You did good out there," she said, looking up at the alien beside her. "This is Tsuzar. The leader of the rebellion that we will be helping with. He will get us up on the Mothership and then we will help him take out their Queen."

"Yes. We have been waiting a long time for this moment. Your resilience is what we have been looking for in a species to help us take down Queen Echidna," Tsuzar said.

"Wait. Echidna? Like the 'mother of monsters' Echidna from Greek mythology?" Ashley asked, astonished.

"The very one, yes. We have been to this planet before, during the time of the Greeks. She partnered herself with Typhon, a blood sucking creature who you may know more commonly as Dracula. Typhon had created a source of food for himself and his kind: humanity. But you turned against him and sought freedom instead of being livestock to the blood suckers. That was thousands of years before we arrived. When we did, the war between humanity and the blood suckers was still raging. Echidna decided to help Typhon and used prisoners she had captured from plundered planets as test subjects, turning them into Vexnoxtuque. You may know them as the Titans. After that, for reasons unknown, we left. Hoping to come back one day to a dead planet, maybe, but we were surprised that was not the case. You survived and we cannot make contact with Typhon. Which is good because the Vexnoxtuque he possesses are the most powerful we have ever created."

"You can't contact him because he's dead. He was killed over a month ago," Angel said.

"That is fortunate."

"Wait, you're serious? Dracula is real?" Aaron asked, flabbergasted at the revelation.

"*Was* real," Angel corrected.

"So, what? Godzilla is real? Vampires? *Bigfoot*?"

"Vampires, yes. Bigfoot, I'm not sure. Godzilla...well...look out there. He is basically our Godzilla."

"Right...I made that joke earlier."

They looked out to the fight between giants. Wraith charged again after seemingly been thrown away again. Bullets and missiles struck the behemoths, but they ignored them and continued their battle. Marugrah twisted his body, dragging his club-tipped tail behind him as he turned. Once she was within reach, he brought his tail up, catching Wraith in the side and sending her flying into the city. Will thought it impossible for something so big to tumble through the air like that but there he was watching it happen. She landed on the International Monetary Fund, the World Bank Group, and the surrounding buildings, shaking the White House roof beneath their feet. Marugrah charged after her.

"We better get going," Tsuzar said, pulling their attention away from the Kaiju battle. "Echidna will figure out what we are up to soon and kill us all before we can even attempt to board the ship."

"Alright. Let's go kids. We have an alien warlord to kill," Angel said, heading back the way they came in.

"She makes it sound like we're the *Magic School Bus* gang with a dark twist," Aaron said, following her.

They took the elevator down and charged through the White House, emerging onto the South Lawn where Tsuzar's three ships were parked, awaiting their arrival. Plagueonians stood beside the ships, ready to jump in and fly off to the coming battle. Tsuzar pointed to the middle ship.

"This is my ship. You will ride with me," he said making his way to the grey, whale-shaped ship.

The inside of the ship was similar to Marugrah's ship. Wide open inside with racks of weapons. Will helped Ashley up into the ship. Aaron jumped in next, followed by the rest of Gamma squad, a few soldiers and a couple Plagueonians. A tap on his shoulder made him jump. He looked over to see Tsuzar holding a laser rifle out to him. Will took it, finding it surprisingly light.

"It works basically like your own weapons. Point and pull the trigger. It has hardly any recoil so it shouldn't be too hard for you to handle," he said to Will.

"Thanks," Will said with a nod, still unsure about the alien.

Tsuzar nodded back and headed for the ship's cockpit.

"Alright," Angel said as the ship ascended into the sky. "Yes, Dracula was a real thing. The man who alerted us to the chimeras in Fresno... well, he actually brought some high powered officials the bodies... accompanied a werewolf in stopping him from releasing creatures of vast power: the Titans. They killed him. He is no longer a threat. But the cult he created is."

"It's just sunshine and rainbows with you guys. Chimeras. Dracula. Friggin' aliens. A cult of monsters," Aaron grumbled.

"One problem at a time," Will said.

He looked over at Ashley. She seemed raring to go. Almost as if she looked forward to the fight. The smile she gave him when she saw him staring confirmed it. Will smiled back, feeling the same way. He did just fight and kill two giant monsters by taking over another monster's body. It was exhilarating. Yet, he was just as scared as he was exhilarated.

He glanced at the others readying their weapons that they managed to keep ahold of. Would they be enough to fight through the giant Plagueonian mothership, though? Will hoped so.

They spent the ride in silence. Once they landed, Tsuzar reappeared.

"We shall go out first. Wait here until I give you the okay," he said.

"Understood," Angel said.

Tsuzar and the three Plagueonians exited the ship,

leaving them alone.

"Anyone consider this might be a trap?" Dingo asked.

"If it is, we're fucked. We're on a ship filled with who-knows-how-many Plagueonians. There is no way we can fight them all off and then proceed to kill Echidna," Aaron said, his voice quivering with anxiety.

"He and his followers killed the attacking Plagueonian force and saved us all. Not to mention President Scott. I don't think he'd do that and then betray us," Eva said, putting a calming hand on Aaron's shoulder.

"She has a point," Will agreed.

The soldiers around them shifted uncomfortably.

The door opened and everyone thrust their weapons at it. Tsuzar held his clawed hands up in the air.

"It is just me. It's all clear out here," he said, hands still raised.

Will peered around him at the hanger bay beyond, seeing the bodies of dead Plagueonians littering its floor.

"Alright, let's move out," Angel said, jumping out of the drop ship and onto the golden floor of the hanger bay.

Will followed her out, Ashley and Aaron following him out. The rest of Gamma squad and the five soldiers jumped out next. Will looked around the vast room. Ships were parked in the space. The walls, ceiling, and floor were gold with alien symbols carved into them.

"Where to now?" Angel asked, looking to their alien guide.

"Now, we make our way to the ship's control center," Tsuzar said, walking toward a door at the far side of the hanger.

The door automatically opened when they were a foot

from it.

"You know, Plagueonian isn't our species' real name. We're actually called Hestialites. Plagueonians was the name adopted as we spread around the universe like a plague, taking whatever we wanted. And that was mostly other worlds. You see, our planet, Hestia, was swallowed by a black hole millenia ago. We needed another place to dwell. We came upon one planet and for a time we lived peacefully with the native species inhabiting it...until Echidna came to power. A bloody war was waged and the natives, a race called *Atlanteans*, were wiped out. We have conquered dozens of worlds since then and many of the world's species went extinct because of us like on that planet...or the only remaining of the species were turned into Vexnoxtuque. Many of our species don't remember because Queen Echidna liked the name so she kept it," Tsuzar said, walking through the open door.

"She sounds like a real piece of work," Aaron said, nervously watching every nook and cranny they came by.

Everyone else did too. They were on high alert. Will knew that was because they were behind enemy lines.

Way deep behind enemy lines, he thought.

"How big is this ship?" Will asked after twisting and turning through the same hallway for about twenty minutes or so.

"Over two thousand feet long and half as tall. It is made to hold the Vexnoxtuque as well as the Plagueonian armada," Tsuzar answered. "But fear not. The elevator that will take us to the control room is not far ahead."

They walked through another door, entering a vast golden and grey room full of...nothing. Half of the room was cloaked in darkness but there was nothing in the room that Will could see.

Until something shifted in the darkness.

"What the... Tsuzar....where are we?" Will asked, something about the shift in the darkness setting off his *oh-shit-o-meter*.

"This is where the elevator is, but... it's in the dark area," Tsuzar replied, just as confused as everyone else was.

"Yeah, well, something is in the dark area."

"It looks like she knew we were coming after her."

"Everyone stay alert!" Angel said to the soldiers and Gamma squad.

The twenty some soldiers that rode in on the three ships and Gamma scanned the darkness with their weapons. Will, Ashley, and Aaron did too. Tsuzar and the twenty Plagueonians did as well. Whatever was in the darkness was outnumbered, but Will had no illusion that the thing had a size advantage. The shift in the darkness suggested something large lurked within. He couldn't determine how big, though. It wasn't as big as the Kaiju he had seen thus far, however.

They didn't have to wait long before the thing revealed itself. Will gasped, realizing what he was looking at when the monster stepped from the darkness.

The Cyclops.

27

The forty-foot creature's one and only eye scanned through the small army standing before it. Will couldn't believe that he was actually looking at a monster from Greek mythology. The Cyclops looked nothing like it had been depicted in mythology and movies, however. Well, for the most part. It looked humanoid with two arms, two legs, and a head. Its face was vaguely human with a very human eye at the center of its forehead and two ears on the side of its head. It even had a nose, but its mouth was much more like a Kaiju's with its sharp teeth showing and lacked lips. Two giant tusks jut from the side of the Cyclops's bottom jaw.

It wasn't as heavily armored as the Kaijus Will had seen thus far. Patches of armor littered its neck, chest, shoulders, and legs. The rest of the flesh was chaotically arranged muscles, much like Plague's. Spikes protruded from the creature's elbows, forearms, and knees.

It twitched its five-clawed fingers, the thumbs looking like spiked nubs. It opened its mouth and let out an ear-splitting roar.

"Tsuzar. I would never have thought you would have been the leader of this rebellion. I thought you were all for the cause," a sinister female voice boomed inside the room.

"Ah, Echidna. So you finally found out. You should have known this was coming sooner or later," Tsuzar said to the disembodied voice.

"I did. And I will make an example of you. This little rebellion of yours will be crushed quickly. My pet will take care of the lot of you. Cyclops...kill them!"

With the order given, the Cyclops charged. The room was filled with the cacophonous sound of gunfire. The bullets and laser bolts hit the creature but it kept charging, a wild look in its eye.

"Scatter!" Will yelled, jumping out of the way as Cyclops brought his fists down.

To his relief, everyone followed his lead and avoided being smeared into the floor. He didn't know how, but he somehow predicted the attack. If he can just continue doing that, maybe they could beat the thing without any casualties.

Cyclops roared in anger as they continued to fire at the monster. Will noticed bullet wounds where there was little to no armor leaking red blood.

Red blood? Was this thing once human? Will wondered.

As horrifying as the revelation that the Cyclops may have once been human, it wasn't impervious to their attacks. That was some good news, at least, but the creature's raging state didn't allow it to feel the pain. Will knew that rage was what fueled the monsters created by Echidna. He learned that when he took over Drakonah.

They spread out around the monster, momentarily confusing it. But then it seemed to understand the tactic. It was almost as if it recognized the tactic.

"Aim for the soft areas!" Will shouted.

They needed to kill the Cyclops soon or Echidna might try to get away.

Will aimed his rifle at the creature's side where there was no armor at all and only soft flesh and pulled the trigger. A yellow laser bolt erupted from the rifle, producing a hole where he aimed. The problem with lasers was that they cauterized the wound so he just hoped he did some damage to the creature.

It bucked and swung its arms under the barrage of bullets and lasers until it had enough. It lunged at a group of soldiers, grabbing one and ripping him apart. Limbs, organs and flesh flew through the air, the scene making Will want to throw up. He kept his stomach contents down and continued firing at the monster as it did the same to another unfortunate soldier.

"We need to find a weak spot," Angel said, motioning to Damen, AKA Wolf.

Will was confused and then was gripped with horror as Wolf slung his weapon over his back and ran toward the rage monster still tearing soldiers apart and even stuffing some into its sharp-toothed maw. Wolf jumped twenty-feet into the air, catching an armor plate on the middle of Cyclops's back. He quickly scaled the creature's forty-foot height, reaching the creature's head. Cyclops finally realized there was someone on its back and tried to reach back and grab Wolf off, but its arms couldn't reach him. That made Cyclops roar in frustration, flecks of flesh and blood flying from its mouth.

Wolf drew his Beretta M9 pistol as he climbed atop the monster's head, unloading the weapon into the Cyclops's eye. The creature's eye erupted in a geyser of red and white liquid, eliciting a roar of pain from the monster. It fell to its spiked knees, clutching its mangled eye.

Cyclops was now blind.

While Wolf was a big man and looked strong, what he did was an amazing feat. It was a *superhuman* feat.

"How...?" Will said, watching Wolf jump down from Cyclops's head, thirty-feet in the air and landing easily on the ground. Jumping from that high would have broken a normal person's legs.

"Damen is...well, he's a werewolf," Angel said. "Hence his callsign."

A werewolf? Will thought, astonished. There was a monster right under his nose and he didn't even know it. *No. He's not a monster. He's our ally...and friend.*

While Cyclops may have been down, it was far from dead. After it was done cradling its eye, it stood back up and sniffed the air. Its sight was gone so now it was relying on its other senses, like how Cerboura did once Marugrah blinded it in San Francisco.

And like Cerboura, it was relying on its hearing and smell.

It homed in on a group of soldiers and Plagueonians, lunging at them. The bullets and laser bolts they fired couldn't stop the monster's rage. It slammed its fists down again like giant sledge hammers. Most of them were able to get out of the way, but a few unlucky souls were smeared into the golden floor. Red and purple stained the floor along with the flattened bodies of the people the fluids belonged to.

"How the fuck are we supposed to stop this thing?" Aaron asked, sounding very afraid.

Will didn't blame him. They were in a very terrifying situation and he was just as afraid, but he didn't let it keep him from taking action. He thought for moment.

"Aim for the eye! Maybe we can destroy its brain," He yelled out so everyone could hear him, but also attracting Cyclops' attention.

"Shit," he muttered as the massive monster sprinted toward him. He took aim and pulled the trigger, laser bolts entering the monster's now empty eye socket and exiting the back of its head. Somehow, it kept charging.

Wolf came out of nowhere, slamming into the side of the charging monster's head and throwing it to the ground. Cyclops cried out in anger. It thrashed about on its back in frustration. It rolled to its feet and slammed its fists on the ground like a pissed off gorilla and charged again. Will watched as Wolf produced a grenade and jumped at the monster again. Once he made contact with the monster's head again, he shoved the grenade into the Cyclops's empty eye socket with a sickening squishing sound and jumped away.

Cyclops grabbed at its eye, trying to find what he shoved inside it but didn't find it in time. The creature's head exploded in a cloud of crimson mist, splashing on anyone close to it.

"Damn. That was brutal," Ashley said.

Will sighed in relief. Without Wolf, Cyclops surely would have massacred them all. Then, Earth would have been doomed.

"Great job, human....er...wolf," Tsuzar said.

Wolf just gave him a nod.

Tsuzar led them past the dark area to the elevator that would take them to the ships control room. And Echidna.

They stepped into the lift, a bigger version of the one Will rode on in the orb ship in New York City. It was able to accommodate all thirty of them, ten being killed by the Cyclops.

Damn. If ten were killed by that thing, I can only imagine how many are going to make it through what we face next, Will thought with fear as the lift rose toward the final fight for Earth.

He just hoped they would make it through it alive.

28

Marugrah watched as Wraith sped off into the city. He had tried to keep it out of the city, but the arachnid Kaiju was resorting to cowardice now. Or did it have a plan? Marugrah had no idea. He stomped after it, crushing buildings, cars, and probably people under his massive feet. Wraith skittered across the Capitol Reflecting Pool and crashed through the dome topped Capitol Building. He knew the building served some significance to the humans, but didn't care about its destruction. His only concern was catching up to Wraith and putting an end to her existence.

He roared after her, the giant bug turning toward his voice as she stopped in the United States Capitol Complex. She roared at him as he stomped across the ruins of the Capitol building, opening her mouth wide, and launching the mass of black tendrils inside at Marugrah. They wrapped around his limbs and threw him into the Russell Senate Office Building. The stone and metal structure crumbled beneath his massive weight.

Wraith jumped into the air, landing on top of him, but Marugrah anticipated the move. It wasn't the first time she tried the tactic. He extended a spike from the chamber on his left arm and plunged it into her soft underbelly lined with tentacles. She threw her head to the sky and squealed in pain.

The pain filled shriek filled him with pleasure, sending him into a frenzy. He snapped his jaws shut on a mass of tentacles, ripping them from the creature's belly. They tasted...good to him. So he swallowed them whole, filling his belly with some nourishment and his body with energy. He went to take another mouthful of tentacles, but Wraith had already jumped away.

Marugrah rolled to his feet, finding Wraith standing in the ruins of the Capitol Building, shaking with barely contained rage. Then she charged, leaving a trail of purple blood in her wake. She jumped again, but her aim was off. Marugrah realized she wasn't going to tackle him too late. Her fangs sunk into the soft flesh of his neck, sending shock waves of pain through his body. He tried to cry out in pain, but it came out as a pitiful gurgle. He could actually barely breathe. Wraith was constricting his air way, trying to suffocate him.

He grabbed at Wraith's armored face, trying to pry her jaws open. She resisted, but she was no match for his powerful arms. He pried her jaws open, throwing her away from him. She landed on her back, but was quickly back on her eight legs. She snarled at him, mad that she could be thrown away so easily.

Marugrah certainly found her a formidable adversary. While the others he battled were easily killed, Wraith was a challenge. Cerboura and Plague were not. He liked the challenge. Loved it. Craved it. And he would win. And when he did...when he did, he would feast upon her flesh. He already got a taste of her...and he wanted more. His stomach growled with hunger.

He felt as if he were starving.

He refrained from eating humans, finding the consumption of the species he was trying to protect revolting. He felt them all around, though. Wanted to eat them. He ignored the craving, though. When he was in the ocean, he turned to eating whales. They tasted disgusting to him. But they satiated his hunger. The monster before him would do the same.

Anticipating the promise of a meal, he charged, twisting his body around and bringing his club-tipped tail around. His tail slammed into the side of Wraith's face, throwing her into the Supreme Court Building, the building crumbling under her massive size slamming into it. Marugrah was right on top of her, clawing at her armored back as he attempted to peel away the overlapping plates of armor to get at the tasty soft flesh beneath.

Wraith shook her head, clearing her mind and letting her feel the pain of one of the plates being torn from her back. She let out a roar of pain and tried to get free, but he had her pinned. She extended the tentacles from her back, wrapping them around Marugrah and sending untold volts of electricity into his body.

Now it was his turn to roar in pain. The pain quickly turned into anger as he sliced at the tentacles with the spikes protruding from his wrists, severing them and unleashing a blast of green fire upon them. To his satisfaction, they didn't grow back. He snarled and continued to peel the plates of armor from her back as she squealed in agony.

He took pleasure in her pain.

He enjoyed her cries of pain.

Her cries soon died down as the last plate was

removed from her back and he tore into her. He ate until his stomach was full of Wraith's white flesh.

29

The doors slid open and they rushed into the control room of the Plagueonian Mothership. To Will's confusion, the Plagueonians in the room didn't seem surprised by the mix of human and Plagueonian soldiers barging in...and neither did Echidna. A sharp-toothed smile was spread across her ugly face, sending chills down Will's spine. He didn't doubt everyone human in the room had the same sensation.

He took the lull in activity to observe the monstrous Echidna. In Greek mythology, Echidna was a half-woman, half-snake monster that was the mate of Typhon. In reality, Will knew that was not the case. They were just partners, making giant monsters to use as weapons. In ways, the Echidna sitting on the golden throne at the back of the control room was kind of similar.

A long, crown-like helmet adorned her head, framing her face that was almost like a skull: red, pupiless eyes sunken into their sockets, her nose looking like a human skull's. Her mouth was all that seemed normal.

Well, whatever you could consider normal for an alien, Will thought.

Her exposed neck was covered in armor plating, like Plague's. Her body adorned a royal looking armor. It wasn't armor like on her neck and the other Kaiju thus far, but more like the armor Tsuzar and the rest of the Plagueonian soldiers wore. Three tentacle looking structures protruded from each side, disappearing behind the throne. Spikes protruded from her exposed shoulders, also much like Plague's. More metal armor wrapped around her biceps and again around her forearms. Her four-fingered hands were huge, being bigger than her own head. Her exposed stomach revealed chaotically arranged muscles, much like the Kaiju and the Cyclops.

Another metal piece of armor wrapped around her waist like a belt, more strangely arranged muscles continuing below it. She wore more silver armor on her thighs. A bone-like structure on her knee looked like a knee pad with a spike protruding from it. Another piece of silver armor wrapped around her calf, a bundle of spikes following after it. He couldn't see her feet as they were obscured from view.

"So, you were able to get past the Cyclops. Well done. I am very impressed," Echidna said, the wicked smile still on her face.

"Spare us your mockery. Come meet your end!" Tsuzar growled.

"Tsk, tsk, tsk, I don't think so. It is not as easy as you have been thinking my dear, Tsuzar. There are little of your rebellion and many of my followers."

As she uttered the last words, the Plagueonians at the consoles stood, bringing up laser weapons of all sizes and started firing. They dove for cover behind some empty consoles at the front of the room, some of them not making it. To Will's relief, his teammates and Tsuzar did make it.

"Fuck! What now?" Dingo growled.

"Now...we kill them all," Tsuzar answered as he popped up from cover and fired off a few shots.

Will did the same, taking aim at the closest Plagueonian and firing, erasing the look of surprise from its face. The alien dropped to the ground, a smoldering hole in the middle of its face. The sound of gunfire erupted beside him, Gamma and the remaining soldiers joining in and dropping Plagueonians. Will could tell they weren't trained soldiers by how many shots they were missing and how easily they were taken out. They were pilots and technicians or whatever worked in a ship's control room.

Twenty more human soldiers were lost by the end of the firefight, though, showing they were just as deadly as a soldier. Their lifeless bodies lay beside Will. The attacking force may not have been trained soldiers but they got some lucky shots in...twenty of them to be exact. Ten of Tsuzar's Plagueonians were lost as well.

Make that thirty lucky shots. I'm going to have nightmares for years after this, he thought to himself.

After seeing people eaten by giant monsters and murdered by an evil race of warmonging aliens, who would blame him? He was no soldier, and even they were haunted by some of the things they do and see during a war.

Will stood from his cover, seeing Echidna still sitting on her throne, that wicked smile still on her lips. *Are those actually lips?* Will shook the thought from his mind. He really didn't care. What he did care about was killing her and saving Earth from annihilation. Saving *humanity* from annihilation.

"So, I've heard my dear Typhon is dead. That is quite a shame. He was good partner. Ever since I came to this planet, I have noticed that he had failed at what he was working toward. I shall kill you and finish what he started," Echidna said, standing from her throne.

"You've been in contact with the Order?" Angel asked, her gun at the ready.

"Oh, yes. And there is someone much worse than Typhon in charge now."

"Who?"

Echidna's only reply was her wicked smile growing wider. They stood in silence for what seemed like forever to Will until someone had enough and fired their weapon. Soon, everyone joined in, firing at Echidna who just stood there and took the barrage of projectiles and laser bolts like she didn't even feel them. Everyone soon realized it and stopped firing. The armor she wore was full of bullet holes, but she herself was unharmed.

"Well...shit," Aaron muttered.

"This...may be harder than I first thought," Tsuzar said.

"Yeah, well, you could have warned us your Queen was half-Kaiju," Will said.

"I believe I did mention she experimented upon herself with the early Vexnoxtuque serum."

"Oh...yeah. Right."

"You consort with the livestock, Tsuzar. You humans know that is what you are, right? Food created by Typhon from apes. He genetically altered ape DNA and thus humanity was created. You were only created for food. That was, until you dumb creatures rebelled and overthrew him for freedom, resulting in thousands of years of war between you. Why do you think the blood-suckers only target humans?" Echidna taunted.

Will knew better than to encourage her taunts by responding to them, but the others seemingly did not.

"So what if we are just smarter monkeys. I'm sure we're leagues better than you, alien scum," one of the soldiers that tagged along growled at her.

Suddenly the soldier's head was missing, flecks of blood peppering Will's face. It took him a moment to comprehend what happened as the soldier's decapitated corpse fell to the floor, blood pooling from his headless neck. He looked to Echidna, seeing a horrible sight. One of the tentacles he couldn't see before was hovering in the air, ending in a snake-like head with no eyes and lots of teeth, the soldier's head inside. He gagged as the thing swallowed the man's head whole.

Then, a thought occurred to him. *Half-snake, half-woman.* Echidna. She was the inspiration for the myth. And if she was as horrible as the myths described her, he'd hate to see what Typhon looked like who was said to have a hundred heads, all of them snakes. He knew that Typhon was actually Dracula now, but he knew there must have been some truth to the stories. Looking at Echidna, he knew as much.

"As revolting as I find you, you taste quite delicious," Echidna cackled.

She smiled again, all six tentacles lashing out. Will dove for cover, hoping the others did the same. A body landed atop him. He craned his head around seeing Ashley's pained face.

"Are you hurt?" Will asked, afraid that she might have been bitten or missing a limb.

"Just from landing on my gun," she wheezed.

He breathed a sigh of relief as she rolled off of him. He sat up in a crouch, still in cover. Aaron, Ashley, Eva, Angel, Wolf, Brice, and Dingo were doing the same. So were Tsuzar and three Plagueonians. He looked for anyone else, only finding nine alive, the rest being a pile of dismembered limbs and gore. They were all that was left of the once forty members they started out with.

"Think you could take her, Wolf?" Brice asked.

"I think she is a bit more badass than the Cyclops," Wolf said.

Will couldn't argue with that. He was right. The Cyclops was a monster, running on instincts. Echidna is intelligent. She can strategize and think rationally. She was going to be much tougher to defeat than the Cyclops.

"Are you going to just keep hiding from me?" Echidna called out. "Fine. I'll come to you."

The sound of a crunching metal sounded through the control room as Echidna stepped on a console, making her way toward their position.

"Shit," Aaron mumbled.

"We need to figure a way to kill her fast," Angel said, jumping from cover and unleashing a barrage of bullets from her Steyer AUG. "Shit!" she yelped as she dived to the side, one of the consoles flying through the air where she was just a moment before.

Echidna laughed, taking pleasure in what was evidently a losing fight. Will looked at everyone in cover, seeing the same hopelessness on their faces that he was feeling.

"No. We're not dying here," Wolf said, answering

everyone's unspoken question. He jumped over the row of consoles they were hiding behind.

"Come to die, human?" Echidna asked.

Will peeked over the consoles seeing Wolf standing before the ten-foot-tall monster that is Echidna. Despite her frightening appearance, the height made her even more scary. Not as scary as the four-hundred-foot-tall Kaiju or the forty-foot-tall Cyclops, but still frightening.

"I'm not the one dying today," Wolf said defiantly.

"We'll see about that," Echidna said and charged.

30

President Scott stood on the White House roof, surrounded by Secret Service Agents and armed soldiers watching Marugrah feast on the now dead Wraith. The alien attack had seemingly stopped. Since the rebel leader Tsuzar saved him and eliminated the forces surrounding the White House, there wasn't one Plagueonian in sight.

The giant Mothership hovered high over the Arlington Memorial Bridge near the Lincoln Memorial. He knew the CCU team was aboard, trying to take out the alien leader. The Plagueonian Queen.

I wonder how they are doing, he thought, praying that they would succeed.

"Sir!" one of the Secret Service Agents shouted.

"What is it?" he asked, all his earlier fear of dying gone for the moment.

The man in black body armor pointed out at Marugrah.

Scott followed the man's pointed finger, seeing three Plagueonian ships approaching the feasting giant. Marugrah lifted his purple blood coated snout from Wraith's torn open corpse and turned in the direction of the oncoming ships, somehow sensing their approach. He roared a challenge at the newcomers.

The ships' only replies were firing streams of yellow lasers at the behemoth. It was an ill attempt as Scott didn't see much damage other than black lines etched into Marugrah's thick maroon hide. If anything, it only pissed him off more than hurt him. He roared again at the attackers, his voice full of anger and unleashed a torrent of green flames from his maw. The ships were able to dodge the flames and regroup. They moved in close together, looking as if...Scott squinted, making sure he was seeing what he thought he was.

He was.

The ships were combining. But they weren't forming a giant robot like in the *Power Rangers* show he watched as a kid. It looked more like a cannon. The three ships combined to form a big friggin' gun! It looked almost like a giant version of the laser rifles the Plagueonians used. A ball of yellow energy formed at the barrel before unleashing a bigger version of their earlier streams of yellow lasers, striking Marugrah in the chest and throwing the behemoth to the ground. It unleashed another 'super laser' at Marugrah as he tried to get up, keeping the Kaiju on the ground but still doing no damage that Scott could see. Every time Marugrah tried to get up, they fired, keeping him on the ground.

"We need to help him," Scott said.

"Help a monster, sir?" Scott's right hand Agent, Deryk

Collard, asked.

"He may be a monster, but he just killed three other monsters attacking my beloved nation and we should return the favor! Now call in some fucking jets and helicopters to blow that alien ship to hell!" Scott shouted, not liking being questioned.

"Y-yes, sir!" Collard said, pulling out a phone as he walked away.

Scott turned back to the action. Marugrah was still on the ground, not even trying to get up now. Out of all the creatures so far, Marugrah had been the smartest, Scott had observed. From what he understood, the Kaiju the Plagueonians used had gone insane from whatever was injected into them and turned them into giant monsters, but Marugrah was able to fight it. However, during the fight with Wraith, he had noticed the creature lose it for a few moments. Especially near the end of the fight.

So, as Marugrah lay on the ground, Scott could see him thinking. Strategizing. Waiting for an opportunity to retaliate.

That will come soon.

The attack team Collard was calling in would create that opportunity for the giant. And he didn't have to wait too long. Fifteen minutes later, the attack team consisting of jets and attack helicopters roared toward the ship, firing rockets and missiles at it. They exploded on the ship's hull, but do no damage. Scott was expecting that. They were only a distraction.

The ship took the bait, stupidly turning to the insignificant human force and away from the real threat that immediately rolled to his feet. They realized their mistake too late. They tried to turn back toward

Marugrah, but didn't get in firing range before he jumped up and caught the nose of the ship, tugging it down with him as he fell back to the ground.

The ship didn't stand a chance against Marugrah's might, but did fire another laser blast, shoving the behemoth into the ground before falling on him and exploding in a ball of blue fire.

"Holy shit. Is that it? Is he dead?" Collard asked.

"Let's hope not. This war isn't over just yet," Scott said, turning his attention to the giant Mothership where the CCU soldiers were no doubt fighting for their lives.

His gaze shifted from the ship to the crushed National Aquarium where Zorax started to stir.

The Final Battle

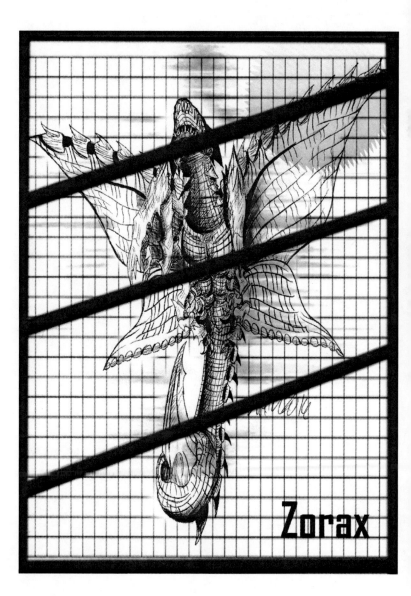

Zorax

218

31

Echidna's fist struck the ground where Wolf was standing just moments ago. If he hadn't leapt into the air when he did, Will had no illusions he would have been turned into a pile of werewolf meat. Echidna retracted her fist, a crater where it struck.

"You're not human, are you?" Echidna asked.

"You're not as dumb as you look," Wolf smirked.

Echidna growled and threw another punch, missing again.

"What do we do?" Aaron asked, pulling Will's attention away from the battle.

"Sit back and enjoy the show?" Brice suggested.

"Yeah, that's not happening," Angel said, giving Brice a stern look.

"We need to find a chink in her armor. Do we have any heavy weapons?" Will asked.

"I have this," Tsuzar said, holding out a pistol looking weapon. It fit in his hand perfectly, but when Will took it, it was huge, about as big as his own head.

"And just what is this?" Will asked.

"A plasma grenade launcher."

"Like from *Halo*?" Aaron asked, eyeing the weapon.

"What is a...halo?" Tsuzar asked.

"Never mind him. How does it work?" Will asked, waving a dismissive hand at Aaron.

"Same as the laser rifle. Aim and pull the trigger. Just be sure you hit your mark if you are targeting Echidna or you may not survive to fire another shot. You have three in the weapon." He handed Will two cylindrical cartridges. "Here are two more reloads."

Will took the cartridges and stuffed them in the pockets on his vest.

"You know any of her weaknesses?" Will asked.

"I didn't exactly get a chance to probe her for weak spots. She would have killed me," Tsuzar said, his tone implying that was a stupid question. Will realized that it was a stupid question.

"We will keep her busy. You use that on her," Angel said, motioning to the giant gun in Will's hands with her gun.

"Wait, what?" Aaron said.

"Let's go," Angel said, jumping out of cover and into the fight, Gamma, Tsuzar, his Plagueonian soldiers and the nine remaining human soldiers joining her. Aaron hesitated but joined them.

"Be careful," Will said to Ashley before she jumped out of cover.

She gave him a smile and said, "You too."

He smiled back, but it faded as she jumped out of cover and into the battle. He feared for her life. He feared for everyone in the room's life. Echidna was certainly a force to be reckoned with and he had seen how quickly she took off that soldier's head. Horrible images of that happening to his friends entered his mind, but he quickly pushed them out and stood, looking over the consoles.

Wolf was dodging Echidna's snake tentacles as they lunged at him, their jaws snapping shut each time they reached where Wolf was moments before. Tsuzar and his men were spread around the control room, firing their laser rifles at her, but she barely even noticed them or acknowledged them. Same with Gamma, his friends, and the human soldiers. Her full attention was on the wolfman.

They didn't even need to go out there. Wolf is kinda doing their job for them, Will thought.

That was until Wolf messed up. He got too close to her and was easily batted away. He flew through the air and crashed into a console, obliterating it. With him out of the way, Echidna turned to the other threats in the room. The bullets and laser bolts striking her body had no effect. They were fighting a hopeless battle. And as Will watched the snakes tear apart soldiers, Human and Plagueonian alike, he was sure of it.

He looked at the giant weapon in his hand, feeling as if it was their only hope. He took aim at Echidna's back, which was facing him, and pulled the trigger. A bright purple glob of energy shot from the front of the weapon, exploding on her back and tearing apart the armor she was wearing, revealing the soft flesh that was beneath it. The force of the blast pitched her forward, but she didn't lose her footing. Speaking of her feet, seeing them for the first time, Will could see where she should have toes, they were snakes, the same as the ones on her back but shorter.

Echidna turned around, her red eyes glaring at Will with anger and hatred. She hissed at him and started in his direction, but was stopped by Wolf who was holding her back by one of the snakes on her back. Will could see Wolf strain as he swung her around by the snake and threw her into a column of consoles, which were crushed beneath her mass. Will hoped those consoles weren't what kept the ship aloft because they'd be screwed if they were as there was no way of avoiding smashing them in this battle.

He didn't feel the ship falling out of the sky, so they must not be the controls, which is good. And now he knew her weak spot. She wore the metal armor to protect her soft spots. He saw Angel glance at him. He motioned her over.

"What is it?" she asked when she arrived.

"I found a weak spot. Get her to turn her back to me so I can get a shot at it," Will told her.

"Roger that. I'll pass along the message."

Angel sprinted away as Echidna let out a roar of anger as she got to her snake covered feet.

"Enough games, primates!" she bellowed. "It's time for you to die, now."

She charged down the clear space between two rows of consoles at the soldiers still firing at her. Will aimed, but couldn't get a shot at her back. The snakes on her back lashed out, taking two human soldier's heads and four Plagueonian's heads.

"I'm not normally into cannibalism, but I will gladly devour the flesh from your bones, you traitors," Echidna laughed sadistically.

Will hated sitting back while everyone else was risking their lives and even dying. He wasn't more important than everyone else. Sure, he was mentally tethered to Marugrah, but so what? People were dying. He'd give his life for the people out there. Ashley. Aaron. Angel. Eva. Dingo. Wolf. Hell, even Brice who made stupid jokes that didn't even make sense. Not to mention the soldiers whose names he didn't know out there. The only thing special about him was that he held the weapon that could potentially kill Echidna. And with her death, Earth would be spared. At least, he hoped.

Will was snapped out of his moral guilt by the *poonk* of a grenade being fired. One of the soldiers fired it from the attachment under his M-16's barrel. The grenade struck Echidna's chest and exploded, throwing her off her feet and onto her back. She roared again, rage taking over her as she slammed her fists on the ground beside her and lifted herself off the ground. The snakes on her back twitched hungrily and more frantically. The rage was taking over her. Will learned what that did first hand from controlling Drakonah. It made you reckless. Open to attack.

Perfect, Will thought. *Give in to the rage, Queen Bitch.*

She did.

She let out another roar, sounding feral and animalistic, and charged. She didn't get far before being punched in the face by Wolf and thrown to the ground.

Damn it. Show me your back, he thought, trying to will her to turn around, but he knew that wouldn't work no matter how much he wanted it to.

More grenades flew through the air, striking Echidna in the chest as she got back up, shattering the armor on her chest and exposing the soft flesh beneath.

At least I don't have to worry about the back anymore, Will thought and pulled the trigger.

Another glob of purple energy shot from the weapon, exploding upon contact with her chest, leaving the skin where it struck scorched. She roared in pain and anger, the scorched skin cracking and bleeding black blood. Another grenade struck her chest, blowing chunks of flesh away in a spray of blood.

Echidna fell to her knees, breathing heavily.

"You've...not...won....yet," she huffed.

"I think we have," Tsuzar said, stepping toward her. He took hold of the long helmet she wore and yanked it off. Underneath was what looked just like the black head band that Will wore to control Drakonah and that Marugrah wore to try and take over Plague. But it looked different. Modified.

"As I said, you haven't won yet," Echidna said, a crazed look in her eyes and a wicked smile on her face. She reached up and pressed a button on the side of the head band. The life immediately drained from her eyes and she fell to the ground, seemingly dead.

Will was confused.

"Why would she just kill herself like that?" he asked, looking at Tsuzar who had a horrified expression on his alien face.

"Oh, no. This is not good at all. We need to get to the ships. Now!" was his only reply before sprinting off.

Will followed after him, yelling, "What is it?"

"Echidna is not dead!"

32

How is she not dead? Will wondered as he helped Ashley into the cargo hold of the ship they arrived in, his thoughts turning to the image of Echidna's lifeless body he saw just minutes ago.

"What do you mean 'she's not dead'?" Ashley asked,

seemingly reading Will's thoughts, huffing and leaning on her knees. They had run from the elevator to the hanger bay, taking half as long as it took them to get there. They were all out of breath, even Wolf.

"That band uploaded her consciousness into a Vexnoxtuque. One of them is still alive," Tsuzar answered, the only one not out of breath.

"Last we knew, the only one still alive was Wraith," Will said, following Tsuzar to the ship's cockpit which was very similar to the Maruian one he drove back in New York.

Tsuzar guided the ship out of the docking bay and back into the night sky of Washington, D.C. and the destruction that was wrought while they were gone. The Capital Building was destroyed along with a number of others that weren't when they left. But the most shocking was Wraith's torn open and seemingly devoured body. Not to mention, the destroyed Plagueonian ship laying in flames not too far from Wraith's corpse.

Marugrah was nowhere to be found.

"Wraith is dead. All the Kaiju are now. So why are you so worried?" Will asked, feeling a little relieved.

Tsuzar was quiet, scanning the city until he spotted something Will did not.

"There," he said, pointing out the windshield...or whatever it was or was called.

Will followed where he was pointing to, his eyes coming upon the decimated National Aquarium where the giant bug, Zorax, managed to right herself, standing on her legs. Her wings flapped, raising her into the air.

"Oh, shit," Will mumbled.

"Where is the Maruian Vexnoxtuque?" Tsuzar asked.

"I don't know. I don't see him anywhere."

"Well, he is our only chance at stopping Echidna now."

Will watched as Echidna, now inside Zorax's noggin, started flying northeast...toward the White House.

Double shit, Will thought.

"We need to distract her. We can't let her kill the President!" Will shouted.

"Agreed. If she does that, nothing will stop her from plundering this planet," Tsuzar agreed.

He angled the ship at the Kaiju, firing laser bolts at the behemoth bug. Zorax stopped in her tracks, looking up at the ship and letting out a screeching roar. An explosion appeared on the side of her face, making her whip her head in the direction it came from. A group of attack helicopters and jets unleashed missiles and rockets at the only remaining Kaiju. Zorax just allowed the explosives to do what they do, taking no damage from them as they pocked her armored skin. She hissed, rocketing toward the approaching attack team. Tsuzar followed her, firing lasers at her.

"What the hell is going on?" Angel asked, appearing in the cockpit door behind Will.

"Echidna's consciousness is inside Zorax. We're trying to stop her," Will answered.

"Where is Marugrah?"

"Nowhere in sight."

"Oh, great."

She disappeared back into the cargo bay, probably relaying the message. Will hoped she told them to hold on to something because it was going to be a bumpy ride.

He turned back to the monster they were fighting as she massacred the attack team. She swiped her pincer-tipped appendages at a Black Hawk helicopter, obliterating it in a ball of flame. Luckily, the pilots saw the attack coming and ejected. Zorax, however, wasn't going to let them live. She lunged up, snapping her jaws over them, swallowing them alive.

Tsuzar continued firing at the Kaiju, the second Plagueonian ship joining in, but she ignored them and continued taking out the human forces until there were none left. That was when she turned on the Plagueonian ships attacking her. She dived for the ship Will was currently on, making him shout in fear of approaching death, but Tsuzar managed to dodge out of the way and get a bead on her within a few seconds. But it was already too late. The giant bug pounced on the ship that was one third of her size, stabbing her tail all the way through it. She grasped it in both of her pincers and ripped the ship in half, spilling out its occupants and debris.

Zorax roared and threw the two halves of the ship into the air behind her, fixing her red glowing eight eyes on the remaining ship. They were the only thing standing in her way.

As far as she knew.

As Tsuzar fought the behemoth bug, Will tried to reach out to Marugrah. He knew the creature was still in the city, he just didn't know where.

Marugrah, Will said. *You there, buddy?*

No reply.

Will knew Maru wasn't dead. He could feel the

creature's heartbeat. He could feel his pain and struggle. And also his determination to stop the Plagueonians, which wasn't over yet.

Maru, Will said again.

I...am here, Marugrah's voice came into Will's head. *Did we win?*

Not yet. We ran into one last problem that we need your help with.

Ah, yes. I feel her. The flying creature. The one you call Zorax. But she seems...different.

Yeah, that's because she is infused with the Plagueonian Queen's consciousness now.

Wait...what?

Yeeeeaaahhhh.....long story. Tell you later. Where are you?

Under a destroyed Plagueonian ship.

The image of the burning ship laying not too far from Wraith's eviscerated body flashed into Will's mind.

Yep. That's the one, Marugrah said, confusing Will until he remembered they shared minds now.

A horrible realization gripped him. If they shared minds, did he see...

Yes, I did. And I wish I didn't. Human mating is quite gross, Marugrah said, disgusted.

Can you get out? Will asked, bringing the conversation back to the matter at hand.

Of your head?

No. That would be nice too, but I meant from under the ship.

Oh... I will try. May take a little bit, though.

Roger that. We will try and keep the flying nuisance occupied until you can kick her Kaiju ass...I don't even think she has an ass...her tail...kick her tail.

Will snapped back to reality. Zorax's face grew bigger on the windshield as she drew nearer to the ship, her jaws agape. Will thought Tsuzar was about to let her swallow the ship, but found out he was actually waiting as twin streams of lasers shot from the front of the ship, cutting into the soft, vulnerable flesh of Zorax's throat. Her jaws immediately snapped shut as she let out a dog-like whimper. Will was impressed by Tsuzar's fearlessness and ability to handle a ship. He was holding his own against Zorax pretty good.

Zorax let out a hiss as she zoomed away in the opposite direction. Tsuzar followed her, firing lasers at her.

"You don't have any Kaiju-killing weapons aboard this thing?" Will asked. "I mean, I'm sure an advanced alien race would have a countermeasure in case their weapons became...unruly. Right?"

"No, we do not. That was Echidna's decision. She probably planned this from the beginning," Tsuzar said, annoyed.

Will didn't blame him. Echidna had manipulated the Plagueonian race for millennia. Turned them into genocidal monsters of war. Who knows what kind of plans she might have thought of. Including this one.

"Marugrah is trapped under that destroyed ship over by Wraith's corpse. Think we could lend him a hand?" Will asked with a smirk.

Tsuzar smirked as well, understanding that their only weapon was still within reach. He cut off the chase with the Echidna-infused-Zorax and sped toward the flattened Capital Building, where the destroyed Plagueonian ship was just beyond along with Wraith's torn open corpse. He fired at the ship, creating a massive hole just as something impacted the ship.

Will watched as the world outside the window began to spin. Before he knew it, he was looking at the ground and then everything went black.

33

Marugrah rose from the wreckage of the Plagueonian ship in time to see the ship Will was on fall from the sky and crash into the National Records and Archives Administration Building. The sight sent rage flowing through his body, sending him charging at the creature responsible for the ship to crash: Zorax. The creature's legs were open to embrace him as he tackled the giant bug. As they fell to the ground, Zorax's legs gripped Marugah's sides tight as she flexed her armored back, flipping so that Marugrah landed on his back instead of Zorax landing on hers. The ground shook under Marugrah's mass as he landed in the ruins of the Capitol Building.

Zorax leaned in close.

You have messed everything up, you damn abomination! a sinister female voice came.

Marugrah knew this was the Plagueonian Queen talking.

I messed everything up? You destroyed my home planet, monster! Marugrah replied with a snarl.

His head filled with a cackling laughter. *Ah, yes.*

Maruia. That was a difficult planet to plunder, but I did and I enjoyed every minute of it.

He let out a roar, unleashing his green flames upon Zorax's face. She squealed with pain, loosening her grip on Marugrah. He pushed the giant bug off of him and got to his feet. He tried to control his rage, knowing that it made him clumsy and reckless, but Zorax didn't seem to understand that. Or the Plagueonian Queen controlling the monster didn't, at least.

Zorax charged, her eyes radiating of anger and malice. He was expecting her to lash out with her pincer-tipped claws, but she instead swung out her stinger-tipped tail which found his thigh. Pain shot through his body, making him cry out in pain. He felt something enter his body from the stinger, but had no idea know what. She could be injecting her babies into him like those creatures from a book of Will's he read. Or the stinger could work like an earth scorpion, injecting venom into his body.

Either one of those wouldn't be a good thing.

There were no offspring ripping from his flesh so that was a good sign, but he could feel something coursing through his veins that were big enough to drive a car through. The venom. He ignored it and retaliated, bringing his own tail around, striking Zorax in the side with the club at the end of it.

She cried out as she spun through the air, unable to stabilize herself. Her wings flapped frantically until she finally gained control again, just feet from the ground, dust billowing up from each beat of her massive wings. She glared at Marugrah for a moment before charging at him. He just stood his ground, waiting for her to get in range. Once she was within reach, he lifted up one of his feet and kicked out, sending her flying...again.

Well, technically, she was always flying, but not in the way Marugrah was flinging her around.

Zorax steadied herself, snarled and charged again. Her jaws ready to rip his flesh from his body. Her claws ready to rip into his armored skin. He never let her get the chance. He leaned back as he grabbed her by the chest, between her back six legs and two front pincer-tipped scythe legs with both hands. Unfortunately, he didn't factor in her tail which plunged into his gut, breaking past the overlapping plates of armor that lined it. The pain made him lean forward and allowed Zorax to sink her teeth into his softer neck.

You're going to die, the Plagueonian Queen's voice came gleefully. *I'm going to rip your throat out and watch you slowly drown in your own blood.*

He felt her teeth tug at his flesh, making good on what she just said, but he snapped his hands up, grabbing her head and holding it in place. He got his fingers around her jaws and pulled, prying her jaws apart. Once her teeth were no longer sunk into his skin, he tossed her away, using the same tactic he did when Wraith tried to do the same thing.

Marugrah roared as Zorax landed on her side on the ground. He stomped toward her as she tried to get to her many feet. She looked up at him, knowing she wasn't going to make it in time.

Until Marugrah faltered.

His body felt weak. His legs felt like falling out beneath him. They did, felling him to his armored knees as his vision faded. He fell forward, his vision going

233

black as he hit the ground.

34

Will awoke with a groan. His body ached. For some reason he couldn't open his eyes but he felt himself lying on his back. He heard voices, but he couldn't hear what was being said because of the ringing in his ears. He felt a tug on his arms and then felt himself being dragged. Cold wind hit his face along with the smell of smoke and fire. He heard sirens radiating through the city and car alarms sounding out mixed with the roars of the battling Kaiju and sounds of battle. There were no other sounds that he could hear. No screams of the dying or panicking. No jets or planes. Nothing.

Maybe the military gave up? Will wondered. Who knew.

"Is he alright?" a deep voice asked, Will's hearing clearing up.

"I checked his pulse. It's strong. He's just out cold," Angel's voice replied, seemingly the one who pulled him out of...

Where was I before I was knocked out?

He searched his memories, trying to remember.

Oh right... The ship... We crashed...

"Everyone else alright?" she asked.

Will heard every one report affirmative, even picking out Ashley's voice from the barrage of voices that sent his head writhing with pain. It told him how he felt about her. It's funny how an apocalyptic situation like this had brought them so close in a matter of three days.

Has it really been just three days? It feels like it has been weeks. I suppose that's what happens when you fight against an alien invasion and their Kaiju weapons.

"The ship is fucked. What are we going to do now?" Will heard Brice ask.

"We need to get to the White House," Angel said.

"How are going to do that with unconscious Will over there," Aaron's voice came.

Will groaned again, his eyes suddenly snapped open, filling with the image of the night Washington sky lit with the flicker of fire. He could see the smoke rising into the sky. He groaned as he got to his feet.

"Well, that's one problem solved," Aaron said.

Will gripped his head which pulsated with pain so intense he almost fell to the ground again but was caught by Ashley.

"You alright, babe?" she asked.

"Babe...?" Will asked groggily, confused.

"Sorry. That just kind of slipped out."

"No, it's alright. I like it."

She smiled. He smiled back.

"You good to go?" Angel asked.

"Yeah," Will said, standing up with a wince. The pain wasn't as bad as when he first stood up.

"Good. We need to make it to the White House."

Will nodded, not speaking his acknowledgment as it hurt his head to talk.

They struck out, trying to navigate what was left of the city. It was hard to do with almost every recognizable building reduced to piles of rubble, many of which they had to climb over. Aaron was cradling his left arm so they had to help him over them. Will suspected it was broken, but Aaron insisted it was a fracture. Will wasn't about to argue with him as he had no real idea.

He didn't know how long they walked through the decimated city until they eventually reached their destination. They rushed across the South Lawn, making their way through the White House, finally ending up on the roof.

"Thank God you are alive," Scott greeted them, looking sincerely relieved. "Marugrah isn't doing too well."

Will's attention immediately snapped to the battle in the distance in time to see Marugrah fall on his face. Zorax crawled over his fallen body, sitting atop it. She jabbed Marugrah three times in his soft side with her stinger. Will realized what was happening.

"She's killing him," Will said, tears forming in his eyes.

"If he dies, there is no hope. For either of us. She will kill us all," Tsuzar said.

"Isn't there anything we can do?" Will asked, desperate to save his friend.

Before anyone could suggest anything, ships flooded from the Mothership, heading straight for Zorax.

"What in the world?" Tsuzar asked, just as confused as everyone else.

"What is it?" Will asked.

"I didn't have that many followers. Especially not as many as I am seeing in those attack ships. Something happened. Something...changed."

"Sir, communications from the ship," one of the two Plagueonians that survived the crash said.

Tsuzar switched on his communication device and was immediately greeted by a voice.

"Hello, Tsuzar, my friend," the female voice came.

"Savernst? What is happening?" Tuszar asked, even more confused.

"Helping in your cause. Saving humanity from the Vexnoxtuque," the one called Savernst said.

"I see that, but you weren't one of my followers. And neither are the ones in the ships."

"Oh, yes. We have seen the Queen's lifeless body. We were afraid to stand against her, unlike you. But with that sight, we were filled with relief. She is dead. We are free."

"Not quite yet."

"Huh?"

"She transferred her mind into Zorax."

"Zorax?"

"Uh... that is what the humans call the Vexnoxtuque."

"Damn her. Always a coward when faced with death. This news doesn't surprise me."

"Just keep her busy and get a team over to the Maruian. We need to get the venom she injected into him out. He is our only hope of fighting her right now."

"Roger that, Commander. I will get a team on it right away."

"Thank you. Tsuzar out."

Tsuzar turned to Will and gave him a thumbs up. He felt like hugging the alien but, he resisted that urge. Instead, he gave him a thumbs up back and turned his attention to the battle that was about to begin.

Hearing the approaching ships, Zorax's head snapped in their direction, letting out a defiant roar and taking to

the air. The ships opened fire, backing away. Zorax
darted toward the ships that started to back away faster,
leading the giant killing machine away from Marugrah
who Will hoped was still alive. Once Zorax was far
enough away, another ship shot from the Mothership,
heading toward Marugrah's still form.

Ashley locked her hand in his, seeing his tension at his
friend possibly dying. He smiled at her, happy for
having met her. She smiled back, probably feeling the
same way. Zorax's angry roar turned their attention to
her.

She dove forward, catching a ship in her jaws and
crushing it. She lashed out with her tail at another,
impaling it and throwing it to the ground where it
erupted in a ball of yellow flames and crushing
buildings. She slashed at two more ships with her
pincer-tipped front legs, tearing apart their engines and
sending them plummeting to the ground where they met
the same fate as the impaled ship.

While Zorax didn't have the twitchy movements from
before Echidna took her over, she still had her ravenous
ferocity. She actually seemed more lethal to Will.

His eyes shifted from the Kaiju to what it was staring
at. Three of the remaining ships seemed to
be...combining. The ships shifted, merging together as
they got closer and closer to each other, forming one
massive objective. It looked to Will like it was a giant
gun. A cannon.

"This happened before...but they used it against
Marugrah," Scott said, staring up at the giant cannon-
ship.

That must be how it ended on top of him, Will thought.

A yellow ball of energy formed at the cannons barrel before firing a stream of yellow laser at the dragonfly-Kaiju. Zorax tried to dodge the attack, but it followed her, crushing her into the ground and a band of buildings, obliterating them all. The ship fired a few more quick blasts at the area Zorax fell, destroying the area even more. Will figured that the quick blasts were to keep her from getting back up anytime soon or an effort to kill her which would have been a wasted effort.

The only thing Will knew that could kill a Kaiju is another Kaiju, which is why they needed Marugrah. He turned to where he knew his friend laid, probably dying.

He didn't want his friend to die. So, he prayed the Plagueonians there could save him.

35

Savernst exited the ship as it landed next to the fallen Maruian Vexnoxtuque. She decided to lead this mission, leaving Maloque, a trusted friend of hers, in charge of the Mothership. The scientists followed her out, carrying the equipment they needed to extract...Zorax's venom from Marugrah's body. She had no idea what to do so she just let them get to work.

One of them pulled a gun-like device out of a crate, hefting it upon his shoulder. The others hooked up cords to it which ran to a glass container. He pressed the gun to the creature's wound, where Zorax injected the venom into its thigh. He pulled the trigger, the giant shuddering as the device began sucking the venom out, the canister filling up with a mix of yellow and green. The gun was relatively silent, though, the sounds of battle in the distance blocked out any sounds it might have made.

Once all the venom was out of the leg wound, they switched to another canister and moved to the wound in the monster's gut, repeating the process. They wouldn't get all of the venom but they would get most of it. Just enough to allow the creature to recover and take care of Zorax. Well, so they thought.

It worked with the one the humans called Drakonah. When they first acquired her, she wasn't pleased. She fought the other Vexnoxtuque, soon succumbing to Zorax's venom as she was 'stung'. They sucked the venom out of her and she was fine. But she was only stung once and seemingly immune to it after her body fought off what they couldn't get out of her. Marugrah was stung *five* times. How the creature was still even partially alive was a mystery to Savernst.

The scientist finished the gut wound and handed the gun to the others. He then began to climb the beast, making his way to the three wounds in the creature's side. Savernst was impressed with the scientist. They were not warriors or used to physical activity, yet he held the giant vacuum gun with ease and scaled Marugrah's giant form with the same ease. Once he reached his destination, he held out his hands and the one holding the vacuum gun threw it up to him, the scientist atop Marugrah catching it. Once he had it, he disappeared, going to work on the sting wounds with the vacuum gun, filling three more containers with the yellow-green liquid.

240

Once he was done he threw the gun back down, one of the scientists on the ground catching it. He then scaled his way down.

"Something the matter, lieutenant?" the scientist who just jumped down asked.

"No. Just not used to seeing a scientist doing things like this," Savernst replied.

"Well, you soldiers don't hang out with us often enough to know."

"I'm a pilot, not a soldier."

"Oh. Well, you probably spend more time in the control room than in the field," another of the scientists chuckled.

She didn't dare scold him. He was right. Most of her time was spent in the control room, piloting the ship. She wasn't a field operative, like the soldiers she talked to. She hardly mingled with anyone else other than other pilots or soldiers. She didn't talk to scientists. It wasn't because she didn't like them or anything, though. She just never came across them.

A boom snapped her from her thoughts, turning her attention to the raging battle. Three of the ships had combined and fired a laser at Zorax, throwing her into the earth. They fired three more short bursts, driving her deeper and hopefully knocking the creature out.

"Hurry up and inject him with the wake up juice," Savernst told them, motioning to the giant, taking her eyes off the battle.

Their only reply were nods and opening another crate. One of them pulled out another gun-like device. The other two pulled out a vial of orange liquid and a glass cylinder. They filled up the glass cylinder full of the liquid and handed it to...she really needed to know their names.

"What are your names?" she asked, the question sounding odd to her.

They seemed surprised she would ask and grateful that she did.

"I am Razerah," the one with the gun device said, loading the glass cylinder into the device.

"I am Charkah," the one who handed the cylinder to Razerah said.

"And I am Frazkrah," the last one said.

They all bowed in unison.

"At ease, friends," she said.

"Friends?" Razerah asked.

"Yes. We are friends now. We all need to grow closer. Echidna had us all factioned out, making us stay separate from one another. Now that she is gone, we must come closer together so we are now friends."

They just smiled at her, not saying anything. She felt satisfaction at what she just did. Tsuzar was a good leader and had been fighting for this moment a long time. But the one thing she kept from them was that the Queen wasn't dead. She was inside the body of Zorax. And the only defense they had against Zorax was Marugrah. Which brought them back to the matter at hand.

She motioned to Marugrah, Razerah nodding. He walked over to Marugrah, sticking the gun device in the giant wound in the creature's gut. He pulled the trigger, the liquid shooting into wound, being soaked into the walls of the wound.

"Load everything up quickly. We need to be gone

before he wakes up," Savernst ordered.

"Yes, ma'am," they said in unison, packing up their gear.

Once they were done, she led them into the ship, jumping into the pilot seat of the transport ship. She started the ship, the engines warming up. Once they were ready to go, she lifted the ship into the air, pulling away from the waking giant.

Once she was far enough away, she watched as Marugrah's reptilian eyes snapped open. He swiveled his head around, trying to get his bearings. He got his arms under him and pushed himself up, standing to his feet. He still looked a little weak to Savernst, but the sound of Zorax's roar seemed to fill him with rage and energy. He whipped toward the sound, spotting the Kaiju crawling out of the hole she made with her body. He let out a huff and charged across the broken city after his enemy.

After all of their enemy.

"Such a resilient creature," she heard Charkah mumble.

"Indeed. And our only hope at defeating Zorax," Savernst said as she watched the creature charge toward the final battle before they will be truly free from Echidna's tyranny.

Will watched with excitement as Marugrah caught Zorax by surprise, slamming his fists down upon her armored back, throwing her back to the ground with a high-pitched screech. Will cheered as he planted his foot on her back, not allowing her to get up. Her wings flapped frantically and she clawed at the ground, scrabbling for purchase to pull herself free to no avail.

She was pinned.

But she was also far from defenseless.

Her tail sprang up and wrapped around the leg that held her down in a death grip. At first, Marugrah showed no reaction, but as the tail began to tighten, he couldn't help but cry out in pain. Will could feel the pain, but not as intensely as he did. Just a dull ache in his lower leg. In fact, he could feel Marugrah's other injuries as well the same way. Along with his own injuries.

Marugrah clawed at Zorax's tail, leaving gouges in her skin so deep that fountains of purple erupted from them and elicited screams of pain from Zorax, but she never let go despite her pain. Marugrah, however, did. He lifted his foot up, releasing her and struggled with the constrictor trying to break his leg. But as soon as she was free, the tail released his leg and she darted forward on her many legs, crawling out of his range.

He put his leg back down, it aching, but at least it wasn't broken. Zorax flapped her wings, taking to the air. Her tail snapped into an attack position beneath her airborne body. Ready to inject more venom into his body.

Be careful. I don't know if you can handle anymore of her venom, Will said, his voice being projected into Marugrah's mind.

I know. I know exactly what I need to do, Marugrah's

reply came.

Will smiled as Marugrah projected what he was about to do into his mind. He did learn some stuff while reading the Kaiju books and watching the Kaiju movies Will owned.

Zorax roared a challenge, her tail twitching in anticipation. Marugrah roared back, accepting her challenge. She clapped her pincer together, starting to look like she was returning to her old self before Echidna took over her mind. *Or maybe Echidna was becoming crazier than she was, turning into old Zorax?* Will had no idea. She threw herself forward at Marugrah, her tail ready to attack. Her tail cocked back and was thrust forward.

Marugrah dodged the attack, taking hold of her already damaged tail. Zorax bucked and squirmed, trying to free her stinger-tipped tail, but Marugrah held it tight. He found where Will bit the chunk out of it when he controlled Drakonah near the middle of it. He pulled, ripping the half with the stinger away. Zorax squealed in pain, blood pouring from the now stump of a tail. Marugrah threw her away, looking at the stinger in his hand.

Will saw another idea forming in Marugrah's head.

Zorax writhed on the ground in pain as Marugrah stomped toward her. Once he reached her, he picked her up by the throat, her mandibles twitching as she gagged for air. He looked at the stinger in his other hand before jabbing it into the soft flesh of her neck. He squeezed the bulb, injecting her own venom into her system.

Will had no idea if she was immune to her own venom or not. If she was, Marugrah would have to find a different approach to killing her.

Zorax stabbed at Marugrah with her phantom limb, the severed end hitting his side and leaving a purple stain. He threw her down at his feet. She sneered up at him as she laid on her back. Marugrah just tilted his head to the side, watching her.

She hissed, snarled, barked and tried to get to her many feet, but all he did was watch her as she did. He seemed almost amused with her struggles. And when they faded, he squealed with glee. Her movements became slow and the snarling stopped. She stopped writhing on the ground and soon became still.

Still not satisfied, Marugrah planted his foot on her head. He slowly increased the pressure, a loud *splat* soon echoing through the city as her head caved in from the pressure beneath his foot. He lifted his foot up, gooey purple and blue stuck to it, dripping strands of goo.

Will almost puked at the sight. It was disgusting. Even more so when Marugrah picked up a chunk of her mashed brain and dropped it in his maw, eating it. Some of the Secret Service Agents couldn't hold it down and blew chunks all over the White House roof.

"What is with him and eating other Kaiju?" Scott asked in disgust, holding back whatever he wanted to spew out of his stomach.

"It's either Kaiju or people," Will said, holding back his own vile spew.

"Ah... Kaiju is definitely better."

The brain was the only bite he took of the monster's decapitated corpse. He looked at it a long time before turning away and trudging through the decimated city.

He was heading back the way he came hours ago, back toward Chesapeake Bay.

Will watched him leave until he couldn't see him anymore and turned toward the people on the roof with him. Ashley smiled at him. He returned the smile. She looked relatively unharmed but was covered in dirt and grime.

He turned his attention to his own injuries. His head ached. Maybe a minor concussion. The rest of his body ached, but it didn't feel like anything was broken. Just bruised.

He looked to his best friend, Aaron. He cradled his arm, but still managed to give Will a thumbs up, accompanied with a pained smile.

He needs to get that looked at as soon as possible, Will thought, concerned.

Other than that, being covered in dirt like everyone else in the crash, and the streak of blood running from his temple, Aaron was unharmed and looked fine.

His attention turned to the team he had worked with for the past three days. They seemed fine. Alert. And happy.

It was finally over.

Zorax...Echidna...was dead.

All the Plagueonian Kaiju were dead.

Even Tsuzar and his remaining soldiers were cheering with President Scott and his agents.

They had won.

But Will still kept his guard up. He was still on edge.

But why? he wondered. *Echidna is dead. Her Kaiju are dead. Her followers have turned against her. So why am I still on edge?*

His eyes went wide as a horrible realization set in.

"Shit," he muttered. "Shiiiiiit."

"What is it? Will?" Ashley asked.

"She transferred her consciousness into Zorax, right? What if when she...Zorax died...it snapped back into her original body?"

"Will...what are you saying?"

"He's saying," Tsuzar said, walking up to them, "is Echidna's still not dead."

"Yeah, her consciousness just snapped back to where it came from."

They looked up just as the Mothership stopped over the White House. An object exploded from the side of the ship as something jumped from it.

The roof shook as the object slammed in the roof, being engulfed in smoke. Red eyes flashed from within as a familiar figure stepped from smoke and the crater she created.

"Time to finish what I started," Echidna said with a wicked smile.

37

"Are you freakin' kidding me?" Aaron asked, watching Echidna, back in her Plagueonian body, step out of the crater she made jumping, or being thrown, from the Mothership.

"You've turned everyone against me, Tsuzar," Echidna snarled. "They threw me from my own ship!"

Thrown it is, Will thought.

"I turned no one against you. They have always despised you, but were too terrified to act until now," Tsuzar countered, readying his weapon.

Will would have readied his, but he didn't have one. He realized he must have lost the plasma launcher in the crash.

Damn, he thought. *It would have been very useful in this fight.*

He looked to Aaron who still had his rifle. With his broken arm, he couldn't use it himself, but Will could. He made his way over to Aaron.

"Hand me your gun," he whispered to Aaron.

Aaron glanced at him and shrugged off his SCAR, Will catching it as it fell. Aaron reached into his vest with his good arm, handing Will his extra magazines.

"Get out of here, man," Will said.

"But," Aaron started, but was cut off by Will.

"You're useless with your injured arm. We'll be fine. Just hide...and take the President with you."

"What about your head?"

"It's fine. Just hurts. *Now go.*"

Aaron stared at him for a few moments before running off. He watched his friend escort the President into the hallway they arrived on the roof through. Once they were out of his sight, he looked to his side, finding Ashley.

"I don't suppose you'd hide if I asked, eh?" he asked her.

"Fuck no," she said, looking offended that he would even suggest it.

"I'm sorry. I'm just afraid we may not make it out of this one..."

She put her hand on his shoulder, making him look her in her shining blue eyes. "We've made it this far. We're not about to die now." She smiled.

He smiled back, but the moment was cut short as an impact shook the roof. He looked to see Echidna pulling her fists from the crater she made as she tried to smash someone. He realized that someone was Tsuzar as he jumped at her, wielding some kind of energy sword. It wasn't like the sword from *Halo,* but was more like a regular human sword, but the blade was made of crackling blue energy while the hilt was solid and silver with alien symbols carved into it. He thrust the blade into her neck, eliciting a cry of pain from her throat.

"You know. I haven't felt pain in so long. Until today. I forgot...how good it felt," she said as she threw Tsuzar and his blade away.

"I wonder if you will like death as much as pain," Tsuzar said as he landed on his feet, his sword in attack position.

They ran at each other, Echidna attacking with her snakes and Tsuzar attacking with his sword. Will needed Tsuzar clear to engage. They all did. They couldn't risk hitting him.

"Hold your fire!" Angel yelled, seeing one of the Secret Service Agents starting to raise his rifle.

They looked at her questioningly, but held their fire. There were about twenty of them on the roof. While that was a good amount, Will knew it wasn't enough to fight Echidna. She was a monster, just like the creatures she used to attack Earth, just smaller, but equally as deadly. He saw it first hand when he was aboard the Mothership.

One of Echidna's snakes lashed out, Tsuzar barely

avoiding it, but he did and was given an opportunity. He swung his sword down, slicing off the snake that lashed out at him. Echidna threw her head back and roared in pain as she retracted the now stump of a tentacle.

"Fire!" Angel shouted, seeing Tsuzar now out of the way. "Focus fire on her chest!"

Will pulled the trigger, the air filling with the crackle of gunfire. Bullet holes appeared in the soft flesh of Echidna's chest, leaking black liquid, but she hardly noticed it. She was lost in rage.

Rage toward Tsuzar.

The five remaining snakes on her back lashed out in unison. Tsuzar was able to dodge most of them but one managed to latch onto his arm. He cried out in pain and brought his sword down upon it, severing it in a spray of black. He pried the snake's jaws from the armor in his forearm and threw it to the side.

Echidna roared again. "I'm going to enjoy ripping your head off! Once I do that, the rest will relinquish this silly rebellion!"

"Are you so sure about that? I don't think killing me will take the fight out of them. I am no leader. I just lit the fire they needed to finally make a move against you. And if it's my head you want, come and take it," Tsuzar said, seemingly enjoying himself.

She complied, rage leaking from her eyes, charging him and lashing out with her giant fist.

"Should we, like, help him?" Ashley asked.

"I don't know what we could do. She's ignoring us. I guess the only thing we can do is sit back and hope he can take her out," Will replied.

"I don't like not being able to do anything," Angel

said.

"You and me both."

Tsuzar dodged another punch from Echidna, lashing out with his sword. It didn't cut her as her hand was covered in natural armor, but it did piss her off. She lunged, opening her jaws and planning to take one of his limbs but he was quick and dodged the attack, bringing the hilt of his sword down on her helmeted head. Will heard the clang of metal on metal from where he stood about twenty feet away.

Echidna stumbled back, dazed from the blow, but quickly shook it off, returning to ranged attacks. The three remaining snakes on her back shot out, striking Tsuzar in his armored chest, throwing him into an air conditioner, obliterating it.

Seeing their commander possibly defeated, the other two remaining Plagueonians ran out with swords of their own, lashing out at Echidna. Annoyed, she grabbed both by their heads with her massive hands and crushed their heads within them, purple blood leaking from between her digits. She opened her hands, their bodies dropping the roof, their skulls shattered within their crumpled helmets.

"You may have gotten rid of the Vexnoxtuque, but my armada is more than enough to conquer a planet," she said, turning to the human threat standing on the roof.

"Probably, but your so-called armada has turned against you. They're tired of your shit. Why don't you get that it's over. You've lost," Will said, defiant.

"I have not! I will get them back in line. First, by showing them the corpse of their leader."

"Tsuzar may have started this rebellion, but his death

will not mean that we will stop it," a voice said behind Will. He turned, seeing four more Plagueonians standing there.

"Savernst? You too?" Echidna asked, looking betrayed.

"I have always hated you. Everyone has. The whole Plagueonian race. All we needed was one new planet to call home, but you became a power hungry monster, needing more. Killing entire species. That is something that is not acceptable."

Echidna growled. "If you all won't listen like the good dogs you are, I will be forced to kill you as well."

Savernst activated her sword, the energy blade flickering on, and charged. She swung out her sword, catching Echidna in her chest and leaving a long slice in the soft flesh. She stumbled back, clutching her chest as black leaked from the wound.

"Very well. Have it your way!" Echidna snarled, one of her snakes snapping up and shooting toward Savernst. Then another. And another.

Savernst did her best at dodging the snakes, managing to evade two of them but the third found her armored arm. Unfortunately, it was the arm she held her sword. She hit the snake's head with her fist, only making the snake dig its teeth in deeper. She looked at Echidna in fright. Echidna smiled evilly as the snake pulled. Savernst cried out in pain as her arm was pulled from her shoulder in a gush of purple.

That was over quick, Will thought. *Kind of pathetic, actually. Is she even a soldier? No. Her armor looks different. A pilot maybe. That would explain her lack of combat capabilities.*

"No!" Tsuzar called out as he pulled himself from the air conditioning unit.

Will could see the anger in Tsuzar's black eyes as he rushed forward, his sword poised to strike. He swung his sword, leaving a wound on her chest that crossed Savernst's, creating an x.

"I am getting quite annoyed with you," Echidna growled, holding her chest once again.

"Likewise," he hissed back, glancing at Savernst who was being tended to by the three Plagueonians with whom she arrived. Satisfied that she was being cared for, he turned back to his enemy.

"Do you truly think you can defeat me?" Echidna asked, her mental invincibility still intact.

"We have already injured you many times already. You are killable."

"Those were mistakes. I shall not let you get any more."

"Your ego is quite big for a tiny minded creature."

Echidna hissed, her snake throwing Savernst's arm at him. He batted it away and charged forward with his sword ready to attack.

Will felt hopeless just watching. He needed to do something. He needed to help. He was just human, though. Wolf was a werewolf, but he seemed tired from his fight with Echidna and the Cyclops on the mothership. *Werewolves get tired?* And their guns would do nothing but piss her off.

Think, Will. There has to be something you can do.

That's when he remembered that while he was still just human, he had a special gift. He was mentally linked to a Kaiju.

Marugrah.

He had defeated *four* Kaiju by himself. He'd have no trouble killing one more.

Hey, Maru, Will thought, contacting the giant.

Yes, Will? Maru's voice came into his head.

What do you think of some revenge?

Revenge? Upon whom?

Upon the bitch that decimated your home world.

I thought I just-

Her mind was snapped back into her original body after you killed Zorax.

I'm on my way.

The sound of an explosion drew his eyes back to the battle. One of the Secret Service Agents had gotten ancy and fired off a grenade from the launcher mounted under his weapon's barrel, leaving a scorch mark in the middle of the oozing x on her chest. Her full attention was on Tsuzar, but that didn't stop her from backhanding the man, Will hearing the loud *crack* of the man's spine snapping as he flew through the air and disappeared over the side of the White House roof.

Tsuzar thrust his sword forward, Echidna barely avoiding having her heart skewered, the energy blade ricocheting off her spike laden shoulder. He spun with the ricochet, bringing his sword around for another strike. His sword struck her armored abdomen, just below the soft flesh of her chest. He immediately jumped back, missing being smeared into the roof as Echidna brought her fist down where he stood a second before.

Before the battle could continue any further, the roof shook. And it wasn't from Echidna's fist striking the

roof. It was like something large was approaching.
And Will knew exactly who it was.

38

Will slowly turned his attention to the side of the roof, where an angry Marugrah, his brows furrowed deeply, looked down at Echidna. She slowly turned her attention from Tsuzar to the giant monster staring down at her.

"What are you looking at, Maruian? You want a piece of me too? Bring it on!" she shouted at the giant, her anger making her oblivious to what was about to come.

Marugrah snarled and reached down his hand with surprising speed that Echidna didn't see coming. She didn't even have time to get out of the way before he wrapped his giant fingers around her and lifted her off the White House roof. She struggled to get free, but her own strength wasn't enough to break free from the much larger and stronger grasp of Marugrah.

For the first time since encountering her, Will saw real fear in Echidna's eyes. Fear of the monster holding her in his grasp. Fear...of death.

Marugrah let out a roar directed at her before enveloping her in his green flames. Will could hear her screams...they didn't last long. A few seconds later, Marugrah dropped her half-melted corpse on the roof with a sickening wet splat. The stench of burning flesh assaulting Will's nose.

"It's...finally over," Will sighed in relief.

Marugrah grunted and turned away, heading back through the destroyed city. Will could sense his relief as well. He had finally defeated the monster that destroyed his home planet. Now, he was off to the ocean where he would spend the rest of his life.

With the danger finally gone and the adrenaline draining from his system, Will felt the full force of his injuries. His whole body ached in places he didn't even know he had. But his head was the worst of them all. He felt light-headed, falling to his knees.

"Will!" Ashley shouted, catching his shoulder.

"I...I'm fine. Just light headed," he told her as she helped him to his feet.

Tsuzar prodded Echidna's dead corpse with his armored foot. Satisfied that she was dead, he made his way to the injured Savernst. The three other Plagueonians patched her up pretty good, though.

Will turned his attention to the city, watching Marugrah wade through the ruined city as the sun started to peek over the horizon. Something wet landed on his cheek. He looked to the sky to see white flakes falling from it.

"Snow," Ashley said with a smile.

A smile spread across Will's lips as well. After all he had seen these past few days -people eaten, shot, or being stepped on- seeing the small flakes of frozen water falling from the sky was actually beautiful. It may be cold and wet, but once it covered the ground and sparkled in the sun, it was simply a magnificent sight.

"So, what now?" Angel asked, turning to the eight-foot-tall aliens massed on the roof.

"Now, we go home, never to bother another planet

again. I want to undo what Echidna has done," Tsuzar said, stepping toward Gamma squad's leader. "It was a pleasure working with you. You are not a bad species." He held out his hand.

"I don't know about that. We certainly have things to work on as a species," Angel said, taking his hand and shaking it.

And she was right, Will knew that. There was so much wrong with the world these days. Religious cults killing in the name of their religion and starting wars. Tensions between nations. Racism. Shootings. Bombings. Bullying. All things that disgusted Will, but they were all were things humanity could work on eradicating, as well. If they put their minds to it...

"Well, good luck on that. We have much to work on, ourselves," Tsuzar replied, glancing back at Savernst who gave him a smile.

"Good luck to you as well," Angel said with a salute.

Tsuzar returned the salute the best he could before turning away, walking toward the group. Will watched as a drop ship ascended from the South Lawn and became level with the roof, the side hatch opening. With a wave, Tsuzar entered the ship, helping Savernst in. The others followed and the hatch closed behind them. A second later, the ship took off, zooming toward the giant Mothership whose grey, alien symbol engraved hull glinted with the first rays of the morning sun.

Will felt an arm wrap around his. He looked to the source, right into Ashley's sparkling blue eyes, her golden-brown hair a mess and waving in the cold November air. Her smile still melted his heart and sent butterflies fluttering madly in his stomach. Even after spending three days straight with her, she still made him feel like this. No girl had ever made him feel this way.

"So, what do we do now?" she asked, locking her hand in his.

"Now," Eva said, exhaustion visible on her face, "we go home."

"Good. I'm going to sleep for a goddamn week after this," Aaron said, still cradling his arm. He looked at Eva with a wink. "Care to join me?"

"Maybe," she laughed, pulling him into a kiss.

Will couldn't help but laugh at the shock on his friend's face. All his advances on the older woman had seemed to finally paid off.

"Wow," Aaron said, a sly smile on his face.

"You lucky son-of-a-bitch," Brice said with a half-smile.

Dingo and Wolf gave him a thumbs-up. Will found it incredible that after a horrible fight like they just finished, and everything that happened, their spirits were still so high. He himself felt good. Not for all the lives lost or all the destruction that was caused. No, his reason was that he knew this was just the start of a new beginning for him.

He knew he couldn't go back to his old life after all of this.

None of them could. They had been exposed to another world they never knew existed.

Monsters were real. They lived among them.

Some may come from the sky. Some will come from ancient history. Some of them created. His thoughts returned to the images...no...the memories that Dal-Un inserted into his mind. The images of the monsters.

Ancient Kaiju. From the time of the Greeks. The creatures buried and long forgotten about. He knew she gave him those memories of hers for a reason.

And that reason was that those monsters were coming back soon.

He had a name for each of the Kaiju. But the name of the group was what stood out most to him.

The Titans.

Epilogue:

A month later, Will stood in the living room of the house he lived in for two years before he was sucked into an intergalactic war from which thousands of lives perished. They still had no idea how many human lives were lost -or eaten- in the events that transpired in only a matter of days. Three days to be exact. And in those three days, New York City, Tokyo, San Francisco, and Washington, D.C. were devastated. It would take millions of dollars and untold years to rebuild the cities.

Even the White House was left in ruins from the Plagueonian and Kaiju assaults on it. Yet, President Scott still insisted upon running the recovering country from it. They had been dealt a hard blow, but Scott seemed to see it as more of a challenge. A challenge to try harder to bring people together. He wanted to patch things up with nations they had...strenuous relationships with and find a way to resolve all current wars. He wanted the world to come together.

As much as Will wanted the same, he knew that would never happen. They were probably roiling in fear, making them even more dangerous than before. Wars would either be waged or just continue. That was just how the world worked.

After the battle and the Mothership ascended back into the sky, never to be seen again, Will, his friends, and Gamma squad were awarded for stopping the invasion. But most of all, Marugrah was commended for stopping the Plagueonian Kaijus. He was praised as a hero, not a monster. It was something that pleased Will. Marugrah saw it all via the mental link they shared. He was just as pleased about not being called a monster even after all he did. He had acted like a monster during the battle and even looked like one.

Marudon, who watched the battle with Cole in the control room, was worried for her protector, knowing why he did it and that they couldn't have won without him doing so, but fearing he would one day lose himself. Will hoped that would never happen.

Will, Ashley, and Aaron decided to join the CCU. After everything that they went through, they wanted to help more. Not to mention, they couldn't just forget everything they went through, knowing monsters lived among them. Once you were exposed to that sort of thing, it's not something you can just erase from your mind. Especially since Will had been having nightmares since then. His physical injuries may have healed, but the injuries inflicted upon his psyche had not and may never will.

I may even have to start seeing a psychologist, Will though, considering the idea. *That might help. I may have PTSD or somethin'.*

Arms wrapped around him in a familiar embrace.

"Hey, handsome. You alright?" Ashley asked, her chin on his shoulder as she hugged him from behind, probably standing on her tip toes to do so as Will was much taller than her.

"Yeah, I'm good. Just saying goodbye to the old place," he replied, caressing one of her soft, peach hands.

"You lived here for a while, huh?"

"Yeah. Lived here for two years. This was my first

house. Bought it with money from being a cashier, too. Kind of a big accomplishment for me." Will laughed.

"Now you're a badass monster-fighting agent. You've come a long way, young Padawan." He heard her giggle.

"You're one too, remember. Plus, you worked at a coffee shop." He laughed, turning to face her. "I'll meet you in the car."

"Alright. Love you."

"Love you too."

They shared a quick kiss before she headed outside to the car they arrived in. He looked around the living room again before walking through the house one last time. It was empty, having moved all his stuff out, which was taken to his new room in the Creature Counter Unit Headquarters. Luckily, the Kaiju that invaded Washington didn't go near where the base was located. Most of the damage was closer to the White House, not near Buzzard Point where the CCU HQ was located nearby.

Having finished walking through the house, he made his way out the door, locking it behind him and leaving the key in the mailbox by the road.

"Goodbye," he whispered to it. It wasn't only meant toward leaving the house. It was also at leaving his old life behind. He had quit his job and sold his house, along with some of his stuff as he couldn't bring it all with him. It was kind of sad to him.

He opened the driver's door to the rental car and got in, glancing at the last of the boxes in the back seat. Jamie and Nicole had taken the U-haul truck with the rest ahead already. They decided to move to Washington as well. Not as CCU agents but they wanted to help with relief efforts for the hundreds of people whose homes were crushed under the giant feet of a Kaiju.

As for Aaron, his arm was actually fractured. He wore a cast now, but that didn't stop him from having some fun with Eva, now his official girlfriend. She was only four years older than him, surprisingly. She looked much older to Will.

I guess that's what war does to you. Makes you look older, Will thought as he looked at his own disheveled face in the car's rear-view mirror.

"You ready to go?" Ashley asked from the passenger seat.

"Yeah. Let's go," Will said, putting the car in reverse and pulling out of the driveway. With a wave goodbye to his neighbors, he drove away, beginning the long journey to his new home. And new life.

And he was ready for whatever was about to come later down the road, knowing it was going to be one hell of a bumpy ride.

One full of monsters.

One full of Kaiju.

He had a feeling this was only the beginning of the... *Kaiju Epoch.*

A Note from the Author:

Dear reader,

I would like to thank you for reading my third book, *Kaiju Epoch,* my first full length novel and my first third-person view book. It may not be as long as other novels, which have 80-90,000 words, but at 61,000 odd words, it's a novel nonetheless. The story has gone through many names and variations in stories throughout the years it has existed. *Kaiju Chronicles* and *Linked* just to name a few. It, like *Blue Moon,* was to be a graphic novel series, but was turned into a novel, existing in the *Blue Moon* universe. And there is a reason for that that you will see soon enough.

I'd like to thank my proof readers for helping me fix my many typos! Thanks Elizabeth Cooper and Dustin Dreyling!

I'd also like to thank my best friend Justin Snyder for helping with story throughout the years we have worked on it. Hope you like what I came up with, man!

I'd also like to thank Garayann Ohme Sutarot for creating the beautiful cover that graces this book. It's simply beautiful!

Also thank you to Jamey Lynn Goodyear for creating the spine and back of the cover! It looks splendid!

And last but not least, I'd like to thank Nick Huber for drawing my creatures for the book. I could easily draw them myself, but I just love seeing how other people put spins on them. Everything looks really great, man! He is but the first of many artists to do art for my books.

Thank you all for reading and please leave a review on Amazon! Also, recommend it to others if you enjoyed it!

About the Author:

Zach Cole is the author of the novella *Tsuchigumo*, his debut work, and *Blue Moon*. He was born in Wooster, Ohio, beginning his love of monsters at the age of two with *Mothra vs. Godzilla*. He became a writer around the age of ten, writing Godzilla stories and even comics containing his own monstrous creations. His love of books started with the *Goosebumps* series, reading anything that has to do with monsters, big or small. He lives in Wooster, Ohio.

Creature Designs:

The following gallery is the original creature concept art for Marugrah, Plague, Cerboura, Wraith, Drakonah, Vishlari, and Zorax, all designed by me, and drawn by Nick Huber.

About the Artist:

Nick Huber is the author, and illustrator, of the children's book *Joe Kitty: The Flying Cat*. He has been drawing since he was five and has developed his own unique style. He likes horror, sci-fi, and kaiju movies.

You can find *Joe Kitty: The Flying Cat* at:
https://www.amazon.com/Joe-Kitty-Flying-Nick-Huber-ebook/dp/B00RC9WNYI/ref=sr_1_1?ie=UTF8&qid=1468983405&sr=8-1&keywords=joe+kitty+the+flying+cat#navbar

And you can see Nick's other works of art at:
http://saintnick14.deviantart.com/

Marugrah

Plague

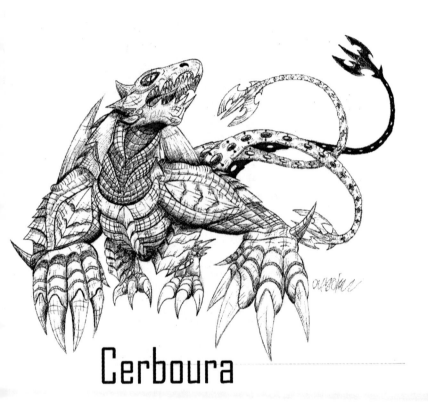

Cerboura

Wraith

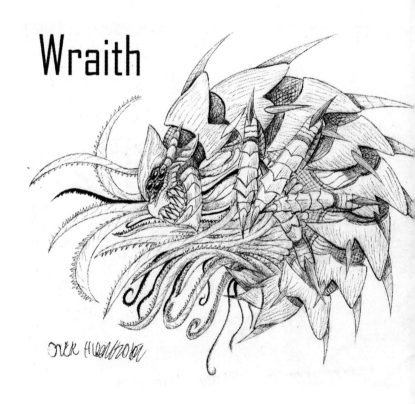

Drakonah

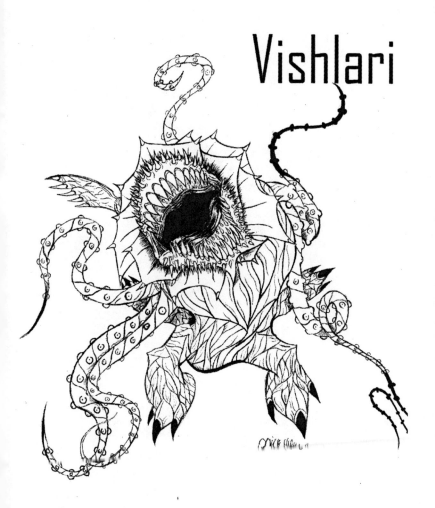

Vishlari

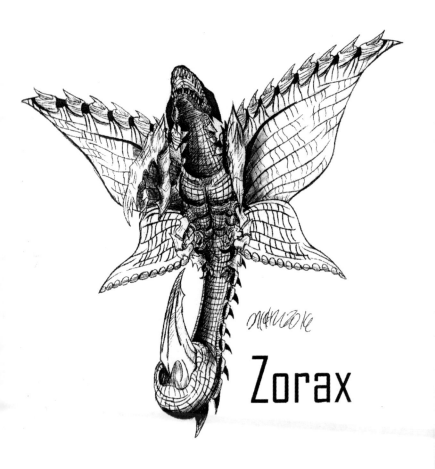

Zorax

Gabe the Kaiju Enthusiast Marugrah Commission:

The following is a commission I had done of the main kaiju, Marugrah, by Gabe the Kaiju Enthusiast. You can see his other works at:

https://www.facebook.com/GabeTKE/?fref=ts

or

http://gabe-tke.deviantart.com/

Marogran!

CPSIA information can be obtained
at www.ICGtesting.com
Printed in the USA
LVOW07s0414300117
522576LV00002B/156/P